MW00982229

WOOLIES AND WORMS

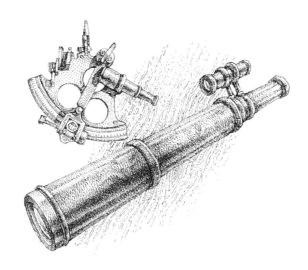

WOOLIES AND WORMS

STEPHEN MacNEIL

ILLUSTRATIONS
BY
JOHN SANDFORD

CRICKET BOOKS
CHICAGO

Text © 2007 by Stephen MacNeil
Illustrations by John Sandford, © 2007 by Carus Publishing Company
All rights reserved
Printed in the United States of America
Designed by Kristen Scribner
First edition, 2007

No part of this publication may be reproduced in whole or in part, or stored in a
retrieval system, or transmitted in any form or by any means, electronic, mechani-
cal, photocopying, recording, or otherwise, without the written permission of
the publisher. For information regarding permission, write to Carus Publishing
Company, 315 Fifth Street, Peru, Illinois 61354.

Library of Congress Cataloging-in-Publication Data

MacNeil, Stephen.
    Woolies and Worms / Stephen MacNeil.—1st ed.
        p. cm.
    Summary: While sailing to the colonies with her father, eleven-year-old Sarah
is swept overboard during a pirate raid, washing up on a strange island where kid-
napped children called "Woolies" are forced to weave fantastical rugs by the evil
Mr. Grim, and those who anger him are cast out to live underground as "Worms."
    ISBN-13: 978-0-8126-2751-0
    ISBN-10: 0-8126-2751-2
    [1. Adventure and adventurers—Fiction. 2. Pirates—Fiction. 3. Rugs—Fiction.
4. Fathers—Fiction. 5. Islands—Fiction.] I. Title.

    PZ7.M2345Wo 2007
    [Fic]—dc22

                                                                      2007014561

FOR REAL-LIFE SARAHS . . .
YOUNG AND OLD

THE *SHY MERMAID*

"MY HUNCH is she won't last," said Captain Murphy, maintaining his balance as the cabin wheezed and complained. He politely ignored Lord Tufts's rubbery legs.

"Nevertheless, I see no harm in seeking shelter."

"M'Lord, the maps show nothing excepting salt water."

Outside the porthole, a surly storm was dumping entire clouds into the ocean, and mutinous waves raged up to the heavens. Seams frayed between sea and sky and day and night.

"Even so, no reason to fret," Captain Murphy continued. "She's traveling naked."

"I beg your pardon?"

"All her canvas is rolled up and tucked away," explained Captain Murphy. "She's a skinnier target for the wind."

"Not skinny enough," said Lord Tufts, lurching towards a bookcase as the ship swelled under his feet.

"Galloping goldfish!" came a voice from under the map table. "So ya reckon we'll end up fish food on the bottom of the wretched sea?"

"Sarah, what are you up to now?" asked Lord Tufts.

"I'm writing down all the sailor talk," Sarah said as she crawled from her hiding spot with a pencil and a battered leather journal. "Father, did you know that a sailor's thermometer goes from 'hot as hellfire' to 'colder than a penguin's arse'?"

"Saints preserve us," muttered Captain Murphy, growing pink around the ears.

"I'm certain Aunt Margaret would be pleased we've found you a crew of personal tutors," said Lord Tufts with a smile.

Sarah believed that her aunt Margaret, a respected second cousin of the king, would have a different opinion to share.

⚓

"Proper eleven-year-old ladies do not hunt bugs," Aunt Margaret had tsk-tsked four months and thousands of watery miles ago. Aunt Margaret held the opinion that grass-stained dresses were a scandal.

Sarah had sat primly on the horsehair sofa while Aunt Margaret lectured Lord Tufts. "Dear brother, your dim view of decency is exactly why the child has not one speck of self-control." At those words, Sarah had tugged at her skirt to hide the fresh rip in her white pantalets. "And goodness gracious, look at those ears."

Sarah's short hair—also thoroughly inappropriate according to Aunt Margaret—meant her ears stuck out like proud young cabbages. But Sarah loved hearing her father say, "You have your mother's ears, and I cherish them along with all the rest of you."

Sarah's mother had died when Sarah was still in her first diaper, and so she had no memory of the woman whose portrait hung over the fireplace. The painting revealed a beautiful lady with suspiciously normal ears and kind eyes that followed Sarah around the parlor. Afternoon tea and the disappointingly bland biscuits were always served under Mother's loving watch. It was also where Father had made his announcement.

Aunt Margaret was predictably horrified.

"Sarah Catherine amongst a shipload of vulgar sailors? What will decent people think?"

⚓

Standing in Captain Murphy's cabin, Sarah had her own opinion. "Your sailors are excellent teachers," she said. "Today they helped me label the *Shy Mermaid*."

Sarah opened her journal to a drawing of the ship. Captain Murphy had supposedly named it after an old sweetheart—

claiming that in his younger days as a cabin boy he had courted a particularly lovely mermaid for close to six months. Sarah had her doubts; it was hard enough to picture some half woman, half fish, let alone imagine the plump Captain Murphy as a small pink boy.

"See, the front is the bow, and the rear is the stern," said Sarah now, pointing them out on her drawing. "The left side is port, and the right is starboard. And this big timber is the mast that holds the mainsail. Oh, and you must remember that the cook doesn't prepare meals in a kitchen; on a ship it's called the galley. I'd be down there now if it weren't for today's menu."

"Troubles, Miss?" asked Captain Murphy.

"Only after your crew eats a meal of beans and cabbage," said Sarah. "I never knew humans could make such noises. The trumpeting is almost worse than the—"

"You made the wise choice coming here," stammered Captain Murphy, obviously not comfortable discussing his crew's gassy condition.

"But now I suggest you return to your lessons, daughter," said Lord Tufts. "Being away from school is no excuse to stop your education."

"But, Father, I haven't stopped," said Sarah. "This morning I also learned to whistle. Listen—" She pursed her lips and puffed her cheeks, but as she blew, Sarah wondered why her whistle sounded no better than sputtering air.

"It's coming along dandy, Miss," said Captain Murphy. "Only danger is, a blast like that could beckon every sea monster within earshot."

Sarah teased, "And do these sea monsters live anywhere near your old valen—"

CRUNCH!

The cabin jerked to one side, and Sarah and her father bounced off the bookcase. The jolt even knocked Captain Murphy off his feet and into a chair. For the first time on the voyage, Captain Murphy looked alarmed, and Sarah could think of only one explanation—sea monsters.

SEA MONSTERS

SARAH GLIMPSED her reflection in the gleaming saber as her father drew his weapon from its scabbard. Captain Murphy tucked a pistol into his ample waistband.

"Sarah, keep out of sight," yelled Lord Tufts over the hullabaloo of urgent shouts and crunching wood.

Sarah nodded as the men raced from the cabin. Alone, she scrambled onto the map table, opened the porthole, and peered outside. Her heart shuddered as an inky black ship scraped against the hull of the *Shy Mermaid*. A flag bearing the skull and crossbones flapped in the howling wind as dozens of pirates heaved thick ropes over the side of the ship. Iron hooks on the ends chewed into the *Shy Mermaid*'s deck, clawing the two vessels together. Pirates swarmed across these grappling lines with muskets and swords. Some clenched knives in their teeth—biting the blade with lips curled back into evil grins.

Swarthy faces and filthy clothes melted into the storm's lashing rain. Only one attacker stood out from the rest—a seven-foot giant crammed into mustard-and-cherry-striped tights. Sarah winced as the enormous pirate lumbered over the railing, clutching a cutlass that could slice through bone in a single swoosh.

Sarah hooked her elbows over the edge of the porthole and leaned out to see her father and Captain Murphy charge on deck while the *Shy Mermaid*'s crew scrambled up from the hatches.

"Cut those cursed ropes!" ordered Captain Murphy.

"Hyenas and hatpins!" gasped Sarah as a beefy pirate flashed a cutlass in her father's face.

Lord Tufts deflected the blow, but the pirate used both hands to swing his cutlass again. The clashing swords shot sparks into the wet air, and Sarah heard the clanging metal above the fury of wind and battle. She bobbed and weaved as if shadowing her father's thrusts and parries—flinching with every strike of the deadly weapons. Waves buckled over the ship and drenched Lord Tufts as he dodged shifting cargo crates. Sword flashing, he retreated across the deck.

When Lord Tufts hit the ship's railing and could retreat no farther, his body slackened, and he lowered his sword.

"Father, move!" hissed Sarah. "You can't give up."

The bellowing pirate swung his cutlass one last time. Lord Tufts skipped aside, and the blade chopped into the railing.

"Yes!" cried Sarah as the weapon wedged deep into the wood.

The pirate frantically struggled to free his cutlass, but the cold steel of Lord Tufts's sword silenced his efforts. "Jump," demanded Lord Tufts, and he jabbed the point of his weapon into the pirate's rump.

"YIIIIIIIII!"

The pirate hit the water swimming, and Lord Tufts slashed one of the grappling lines as another pirate zeroed in on him.

"Father, watch yourself!" squeaked Sarah.

Sarah ducked as a musket ball whizzed through the porthole and shattered a rum bottle on Captain Murphy's shelf. She dropped to the floor and checked to make sure that her ears were still attached as she watched the amber liquid soak into some star charts. "Who do those bullies think they are?" she fumed.

Sarah wiggled across the cabin floor on her stomach. At the door she peered both ways before scooting down the passage. The grunts and cries of battle grew louder, and she tried to close her nose against the stench of burnt musket powder. Reaching a short ladder that led to the deck, Sarah stepped onto the first rung.

A musket blast followed by a painful wail made her hesitate long enough to grab a nearby scrub mop before scurrying up the ladder. Salt water dripped through the planks as Sarah used her shoulder to push open the hatch.

"Hippos and haberdashers!"

Sarah popped up eye level with a pair of mustard-and-cherry-striped tights stuffed into the biggest leather boots she had ever seen.

"Captain Black Tooth!" hollered the gaudy giant. "I found a young'un." His meaty paw reached for Sarah, but she mashed her mop into his teeth. "Why'd you do that?" slurred the pirate through a mouthful of string. "I wasn't playing rough—"

Sarah smacked the pirate's left ear so hard that the mop handle snapped in two—

"YOWWW!"

And stabbed the jagged wood into a stripe of mustard on the pirate's right calf.

"AHHHHHHHHHHHHH!"

The giant clutched his ear and bloody shin as he clumsily hopped on one foot. Sarah rolled from the hatch as four hundred pounds of pirate crashed down the ladder. She darted across the flooded deck and hid among several crates sloshing about. Cautiously poking her head above a bobbing crate, Sarah searched for her father in the swirl of fighting men.

"Who's flapping on about wee young'uns?" demanded a raspy voice.

"It was Bear, Cap'n," growled another pirate.

Sarah risked one more glance over the crates and instantly regretted it. Six feet away lurked a repulsive young pirate that Sarah guessed to be Captain Black Tooth. A patch covered his left eye, but his right eye shone with murder. His belly, jiggling with tattooed snakes and dragons, spilled over his belt. More dragons roamed Black Tooth's bulging arms while tattooed flames licked his neck. Unwashed skin gave the illusion of smoke and soot swirling around the fire-breathing creatures.

Black Tooth jumped onto a crate and yelled at his men. "Full-growns is useless. Slaughter 'em all!"

Another wave rose over the rails and broke into hissing foam that threatened to scatter Sarah's nest of crates.

CRAAAAACCCK!

Splintering wood thundered, and Sarah spotted the mast as it snapped in half and crashed within inches of her father. His royal blue coat shone bright through the gray sheets of rain.

"So that's why she's flying a royal rag," snarled Black Tooth, and Sarah knew he meant the *Shy Mermaid*'s flag with the king's coat of arms.

Lord Tufts crouched low and retrieved something from the deck. At that moment a big-bellied pirate leapt over the fallen mast and attacked Sarah's father. Lord Tufts's shoulder blow lifted the chubby pirate off the deck and launched him spinning and tripping over a grappling line. Sarah swore she saw something shiny sticking from his side as the round pirate flipped backward over the railing.

Lord Tufts hacked at a grappling line, unaware that Black Tooth had leapt from the crate and charged.

Sarah opened her mouth to yell.

"UMMPF!"

A shifting crate slammed her to the deck and knocked the wind from her lungs. She felt as if she'd been trampled by a bull. Helplessly, Sarah watched the dragons and serpents slither on Black Tooth's flesh as he rushed towards her father's exposed back. The pirate raised his cutlass—

"Behind you, M'Lord!" roared Captain Murphy.

The air rushed back into Sarah's lungs as her father dropped to his knees, saving himself from the deathblow. He clutched a bloody gash on his arm as Captain Murphy hurried to the rescue.

WHAM!

A crate swished across the deck, hammering Captain Murphy into the railing. Sarah rushed to her father as the captain crumpled into a heap.

Black Tooth raised his cutlass to the skies and plunged it towards Lord Tufts's bare neck.

"Don't you dare hurt my father!" cried Sarah.

Black Tooth's blade froze.

"Sarah, get back to your cabin," pleaded Lord Tufts.

"Well, ain't you a prize?" Black Tooth grinned.

"You don't frighten me," said Sarah, but she stepped back at the sight of Black Tooth's rotting teeth.

"Sarah, please, run back to—"

Sarah never heard the rest of her father's words because at that moment a huge wave swept across the deck, washed her over the railing, and slapped her into the icy sea.

The churning water distorted what little light there was, and above her, images shrank and mushroomed and dissolved. Sarah even imagined seeing the pirate captain and the mustard-and-cherry-striped giant swinging back to their ship before the wave released her long enough for half a breath.

"FATHER!"

Hard rain and boiling seas blinded Sarah.

"FATHER! FA—"

Just then a wave force-fed her a bucket of salt water and jerked her down. Pressure on her ears dulled distant sounds, and she heard her father's cries as if through wool.

WATERY GRAVE

SARAH'S CLOTHING drank in the water and clung like heavy armor, dragging her to the ocean's floor. She hastily stripped off her bell skirt and shimmied out of the crinoline petticoat that supported it. She pawed at her suffocating jacket, but it sucked tightly against her body. Sarah quickly undid the first of five buttons.

She strained to hold her breath as air bubbles snuck from her nose and deserted her. She popped the second and third buttons and fumbled with the fourth. Unbearable cold numbed her fingers. Sarah's lungs screamed. Two more buttons to go. Wildly she ripped at her jacket, pulling and twisting and stretching it from her body.

Pop!

The final two buttons floated away, and she peeled off the deceitful garment. Down to her blouse and pantalets, Sarah kicked for the surface with her lungs about to explode.

Swimming upwards, she swerved around debris from the battle—oil lantern, rope, canvas sheet, big-bellied pirate.

"BLAAAGLUGAABLAA!"

The garbled scream was Sarah's last remaining oxygen. The dead pirate's limp arms tangled with hers, and red clouds oozed from the dagger sticking from his ribs. Teeth clenched, Sarah scratched and thrashed and kicked herself free. Her chest burned, her limbs ached, her eyes bulged, and finally, with one last desperate effort, she reached the surface.

Gulping air into her lungs, Sarah rode up and down the liquid mountains as they soared and vanished around her. She caught only glimpses of the *Shy Mermaid* from the highest peaks. "Father! Father! I'm right here," she cried, but the sea drowned out her words. The next swelling wave revealed an even more alarming view—fifty yards away the pirate ship bore down on her.

"Ahhhhhhhhh!"

The big-bellied pirate bobbed to the surface, and no matter how madly Sarah shoved at him, the sea kept pushing her and the corpse back together. "A dead pirate can't harm me," she told herself. But knowing that a shipload of live pirates could do plenty of damage, she filled her lungs and slipped below the water.

The pirate's belly was more than big enough to hide Sarah, and holding on to the dagger sticking from his side made it easy for her to stay in place. She tried to avoid the dead pirate's cold eyes, but they seemed to stare right at her. His round mouth gave the impression that a knife stuck between his ribs had been a total surprise.

Needing more air, Sarah squeezed her head close to the pirate's armpit. Her nose and lips cleared the surface, and she snuck a breath.

Below the surface, Sarah's eyes bulged as the pirate ship's black hull—a hundred-foot blade of chipped paint and barnacles—churned by within inches. She hugged the dead pirate for dear life as they flopped about in the turbulence.

When the wake finally calmed and Sarah left the shelter of the belly, the black ship was already a speck on the horizon and the *Shy Mermaid* had disappeared. Sarah wondered how long she could tread water.

PRECIOUS CARGO

"OY, BEAR!" yelled Stinger from his crow's-nest high atop the pirate ship. "They's got a crippled mizzenmast."

Hunkered over the starboard railing, Bear squinted past the rain, distracted by the fresh memory of the ship nearly cutting Keg Belly in two. He shivered at the thought of his own corpse sinking into the vast ocean. Bear hoped he would die in his sleep . . . but not for a while. Thoughtfully, he rubbed the bloody rip on the leg of his favorite tights.

"Poor child looked so sweet," mumbled Bear as he cupped his sore ear and recalled how she had wielded the mop handle like an angry assassin.

"Oy, Bear! It's the mainmast, so they's going nowhere."

Bear stood up and began to wipe the rain from his face. He

stopped in midstroke, his mouth still smarting from the girl's mop. Lumbering across the deck, he exercised his tender jaw and recalled happier days when he had worked as a ship's painter on a merchant ship. But that was before Black Tooth had seized the vessel and flung his captain overboard. Black Tooth had allowed Bear to choose between the gangplank or a job as a pirate. Bear had made a very fast decision.

His new pirate captain had felt the festive candy-apple-red and buttercup-yellow ship did not put fear in men's hearts, and so he ordered Bear to paint every last surface black.

The ship's previous name, *London Girl,* was also judged not menacing enough for their profession, and Bear's paintbrush fixed that problem, too. Bear changed a few letters and found himself sailing the seas on a big black *London Gorilla.*

Bear shuffled into his captain's cabin where, like a volcano on legs, Black Tooth lurched about too upset to speak. Other pirates waited with heads bowed; at that moment they found their boots incredibly interesting.

Bear couldn't help noticing that Black Tooth's cluttered mess looked nothing like the orderly precision of the ship's previous captain. The cabin was an avalanche of empty bottles, dirty dishes, crumpled sea charts, and smelly laundry. A birdcage swinging from the ceiling contained one scrawny green parrot and two years' worth of its droppings.

Bear sadly shook his jowls and reported in hushed tones. "They ain't following us, but the bad news is, Keg Belly is taking his last swim."

Black Tooth ripped off his eye patch and hurled it to the floor. "The bad news is we come back empty-handed," he seethed in a low whisper, glaring at his men through two glittering eyes that saw everything. "Did you reckon we was there for a tea party?"

"Tea party! Tea party!" squawked the parrot.

"Did you reckon I do this for the goodness of me health?"

"Me health! Me health!"

"Well, I reckon the whole lot of you is pitiful bums."

"Pitiful—"

"Shut up, you bleeding bird!" snapped Black Tooth, and the parrot covered its head with a wing. Black Tooth returned to whispering. "You dimwits couldn't find your own shadow on a sunny day."

This puzzled Bear. "But it wasn't sunny."

SMACK!

Bear reeled from a stinging cuff to the head. Unfortunately, Black Tooth had hit the same ear battered by the girl's mop.

"Shhh—you want them things waking up?"

"Not me, Cap'n," whispered Bear, shielding himself from the next smack.

"Whole trip's been miserable," whispered Black Tooth as he resumed pacing. "It ain't even close to a full order."

"We got three," said Bear.

"Three ain't enough!" yelled Black Tooth, swinging around before Bear could duck.

SMACK!

"Waaaaaaaah!"

Bear rubbed his throbbing ear and winced as the cabin filled with the cries of startled babies.

Beside a fifty-pound bag of birdseed sat a wooden box with three wailing babies. Bear could see that the first had rosy cheeks and strawberry hair. The second was a deep copper color with tight black curls, and the third had almond eyes and skin that made him look as if he had been dunked in honey. Bear watched their quivering tonsils as all three babies exercised their healthy lungs.

"Look what you done now, you buffoon," moaned Black Tooth. "I hope you're happy."

"Happy! Happy!" echoed the parrot, and Black Tooth hurled a plate that missed the cage and shattered on the wall.

"WAAAAAAAAAAAAAAAAAAAH!"

⚓

Meanwhile, drifting with the current, Sarah lay perched atop her first bit of good luck; she'd found a large crate that had washed off the deck of the *Shy Mermaid*. Her second bit of good luck was that the storm had blown itself out.

Everywhere she looked, a limitless gray ocean reflected a limitless gray sky. Infinite gray. Meandering about the empty ocean, Sarah pondered the many dangers of being lost at sea—drowning, shark attack, sunstroke, dehydration. She remembered the crew's story of finding a sailor in a stray lifeboat. Driven insane by the baking sun, the man had guzzled salt water until his swollen tongue had clogged his own throat. Fortunately, Sarah wasn't thirsty . . . yet.

Sarah tightened her grip as the water darkened and a massive shadow slipped beneath her crate. The form, over two *Shy Mermaid*s long, circled back and glided past her right side. Recognizing a whale from one of her schoolbooks, Sarah relaxed only enough to breathe again. The book had stated that whales eat microscopic plants and organisms and nothing ever bigger than shrimp. Sarah hoped the whale had read the same book. Unimpressed with Sarah and her crate, the mighty mammal flapped its tail and coasted from sight.

As the lonely voyage dragged on, a damp mist grew into a thick fog, and time became just as hazy. Sarah recalled the hours zooming by when she had hunted bugs in the garden, but when seated on a hard chair in Aunt Margaret's parlor, each fat minute took the full sixty seconds to waddle past. Sarah found herself dreaming of dry land, dry clothing, and even dry tea biscuits. However, when she licked her dry lips, she yearned for a wet glass of fresh water.

Gradually Sarah detected a new sound—the sound of the ocean finally running out of room. She still couldn't see through the fog, but breaking waves rumbled and the ride grew rougher.

Without warning, the crate surged up and pitched Sarah into the swirling surf. She flailed her way to the surface in time to see her crate smash against giant boulders.

CRABS AND CANNONS

THE WORLD lay covered in rolling fog, and the screech of an unseen sea gull hung in the dull air. Washed ashore as if spewed from a whale's blowhole, a lifeless Sarah lay coated in sand and seaweed. Waves lapped at her feet—one shoed, one bare.

A small blue crab inched its way across Sarah's shoulder as if deciding whether she were edible or not. A soggy blouse seemed unappetizing, but climbing to Sarah's cheek, the crab gripped a tender nostril in its claw and squeezed.

"YEEEOOOW!"

Sarah shot to her feet, rubbing her nose, as the crab dropped to the ground and scurried sideways beneath a rock.

"You should be ashamed of yourself," said Sarah. "That's a horrid way to wake somebody up."

Finding no damage to her nose and seeing the frazzled crab digging deeper into the sand, Sarah relented. "Well, surely you'll agree it was a rude welcome."

Sarah remembered the first time that the ship's cook had served crabs for supper. She had balked at the sight of hard shells, spidery legs, and gooey eyes, but one bite of juicy meat had changed her mind. Now, feeling guilty for wolfing down three helpings at that meal, Sarah conceded, "But I guess it's equally disturbing when your dinner jumps off the plate."

Leaving the crab to its rock, Sarah surveyed the bleak landscape. Her splintered crate littered the shore, but the fog melted away any details. Within a few steps, Sarah realized that one missing shoe was worse than two, so she kicked off her remaining footwear.

A feeling of dread crept over her as she hiked up the hill that sheltered this strip of beach. The barren surroundings made it impossible for her to pretend this was another adventure in the garden. She felt lost and alone. Wishing that her father were there only made her eyes blur with tears.

It helped to imagine Aunt Margaret tut-tutting, "A Tufts rises above adversity." And Sarah even smiled as she pictured her aunt maintaining perfect posture while sashaying barefoot through the fog.

By the time Sarah reached the top of the hill, the fog had thinned enough for her to look down at a shantytown of dilapidated shacks. A faded sign hung from a termite-pocked post that sagged into the weeds. "COAL ISLAND," spelled out the crude letters. "NO TRESPASSING. GO AWAY." Sarah figured the sign must have worked; the shacks looked as if they had been deserted for years.

Beyond the abandoned shantytown, a pier jutted into a natural harbor. The pier stood on massive timbers that allowed the ocean to wash back and forth below.

"Tigers in teapots!" gasped Sarah.

The black pirate ship lay anchored in the harbor.

Sarah scurried down the hill, darting from shrub to shrub, and at the bottom she dashed under the pier. Mud sucked at her toes as she crept through the shallow water. Upon close inspection, she realized that this weather-beaten pier was almost crumbling into the sea. The rotting timbers were coated in green sludge and dotted with barnacles.

Above her, through warped and missing planks, Sarah saw two mangy dogs and four even mangier men. The mustard-and-cherry-striped pirate seemed determined to make friends with the dogs, who strained at their leashes and bared their teeth. Bear held out his very large hand to be sniffed, but the dogs only growled louder.

Nearby, the pirate captain Black Tooth handed a baby to a skittish young man with an unambitious mustache. Sarah watched the weaselly man accept the baby at arm's length.

"Put a hand behind its head," barked the fourth person, an ill-tempered old man supervising the transaction. "Nigel, you gotta support its neck."

"Blimey, Pa," whined Nigel. "He's handing it to me funny."

"And you're handing us a load of bullocks," protested Black Tooth.

"You got it spun all about," argued Nigel.

"Do not," countered Black Tooth.

"Do too."

"Just get on with it," snapped Nigel's father. "And quit waving your mitts round them mutts, you overgrown fool!"

"Sorry, sir, Mr. Grim, sir," sputtered Bear, stuffing his hands into his pockets.

Sarah took slow, quiet steps until the water reached her waist. Fascinated with this sinister group, she positioned herself to better follow the action above her. She watched Nigel adjust his grip on the baby's neck as Mr. Grim watched for more slip-ups. An ocean breeze scattered Mr. Grim's stringy white hair, and the old man stroked his beard until he found a hard bit in it. Mr. Grim pried the item loose, turned it over in his fingers, and popped it into his mouth. Queasy, Sarah hoped the man was eating a raisin.

Nigel wrapped the blissful, gurgling baby in a woolen blanket and loaded it beside two other babies in a rusty wheelbarrow.

"That's it, that's all you're good for?" asked Nigel, glaring at Black Tooth.

"Nothing's wrong with what I brung you," said Black Tooth, raising his chin.

"The order was four," said Nigel, raising his voice.

Black Tooth squawked even louder. "What difference is one screamin' baby?"

"Nothing!" yelled Nigel. "When you can't count!"

"You'll be counting my fists," hollered Black Tooth as he stepped towards the smaller man.

Twitching and jittering, Nigel slid behind Mr. Grim and found his normal voice. "He said four."

Facing Mr. Grim, Black Tooth became more accommodating. "How about a wee girl?"

"You know the rules," said Nigel. "Only babies."

"Shame about that," said Black Tooth. "The girl was royalty. Nearly had the little nipper but—"

"A royal girl?" asked Nigel, and Sarah cringed at being the topic of conversation.

"Is you deaf?" asked Black Tooth.

Nigel nervously groomed his mustache. "A ship traveling under the king's flag and you attacked her?"

"Of course I attacked her. I'm a pirate." Black Tooth was hollering again. "What'd you take me for, a bloody fisherman?"

Sarah couldn't believe the speed of Mr. Grim. In a flash, the old man grabbed Black Tooth's ear and twisted it.

"Imbecile!" hissed Mr. Grim as the pirate shrieked in pain. "They discover what we're up to, and we'll all be hanging from a rope."

"I was just doin' me job," insisted Black Tooth.

"Don't talk back to your father," snarled Mr. Grim.

"Please, Pa," whimpered Black Tooth.

"Why don't you dust off that brain of yours and try using it?" said Mr. Grim, giving Black Tooth's ear a final rotation before releasing it.

"Speak of the devil!" exclaimed Nigel, pointing out to sea.

Through a break in the fog, Sarah spied the *Shy Mermaid* limping towards the island, and she quickly covered her mouth with both hands. Not trusting herself to be silent, Sarah squeezed her cheeks and used all her will power to keep from screaming and running from her hiding spot.

"What do you say for yourself now, half-wit?" said Mr. Grim.

"Why not just kill the fancy pantses?" asked Black Tooth, keeping his ears a safe distance from his father.

"Royalty is like stinking flies," said Mr. Grim. "Kill one and it only attracts more. Now get out of my sight."

Mr. Grim's scowl sent Black Tooth stomping down the ladder on the other side of the pier. Bear hustled after his captain.

Sarah pressed deeper into the shadows as twenty feet away the two men clambered into their waiting rowboat.

"Three babies, four babies, nothing ever pleases him," grumbled Black Tooth. Plopping himself into a seat, he made no effort to help Bear untie the rowboat or ready the oars.

Above the creaking and dipping of Bear's oars, Sarah heard Nigel's complaint, "Why can't I ever be the pirate?"

"'Cuz your brother's older, that's why. Now make it look good," commanded Mr. Grim. "I don't want royalty thinking I rub shoulders with pirates. You hear me, boy?"

"I hear you, Pa," pouted Nigel, and he clomped his way to the far end of the pier where a pyramid of cannonballs sat beside a long cannon pointing out to sea.

Mr. Grim retrieved the wheelbarrow of babies and left Nigel straining to roll a lead ball down the muzzle of the cannon. Sarah didn't make a ripple as the old man passed overhead clucking to his wheelbarrow. "Hello there, you little wittle rascals," cooed Mr. Grim. "Too bad you can't stay so cute forever."

With Mr. Grim marching from the pier, Nigel muttered to himself as he chipped at a flint to light the cannon's fuse. It struck Sarah as odd how fast the jealous son's attitude changed when the fuse finally smoked and sizzled. Nigel gleefully waved at his brother rowing back to the *London Gorilla*.

KABOOM!

Sarah covered her ears and strained to find the cannonball in the sky. It arced high in the air and plummeted right at Black Tooth and Bear.

"NOOOOOOOO!"

A wave of seaweed swamped Black Tooth's rowboat, and a fish flopped across his lap. Sarah wondered why the other pirates on the deck of the *London Gorilla* showed no concern. The pirate crew casually went about their business as if a cannonball raining down on their captain were the most normal thing in the world.

Seeing Nigel lugging another cannonball, Bear furiously rowed as Black Tooth screamed at his crew. "Return fire! Return fire! You know the drill, you ninnies."

Black Tooth's crew scurried about the deck, and amid shouts and curses, a gunport opened and a cannon barrel rolled from the side of the *London Gorilla*.

KABOOM!

Nigel's cannon fired first, and another of his cannonballs sailed over Black Tooth's head and splashed harmlessly in open water.

On the *London Gorilla,* the mouth of a cannon flashed red.

KABOOM!

Sarah's ears rang as the pirates' cannonball screeched over the pier and slammed into the deserted shantytown where a shack exploded in a shower of wood.

Sarah left the shadows and quietly waded to an ancient row-boat tethered to the pier. Slipping aboard the rocking tub, she began untying the rope's coarse knot.

DOG FOOD

B<small>EYOND</small> SARAH'S sight, still laboring in the fog, the *Shy Mermaid* crept towards the island. With a damaged mast, a frustrated Captain Murphy coaxed what little power he could from the remaining sails. Still, he knew his troubles couldn't compare to his passenger's. Lord Tufts leaned over the railing and continued searching the water for any sign of his daughter.

Captain Murphy scanned the approaching island, but his telescope mostly magnified the fog. Occasionally he heard a cannon's muffled boom. "Can't see past your eyelashes in this soup," he reported. "Yet it sure sounds like them rats aren't making any friends."

"The current flows directly to it," said Lord Tufts in a

determined voice. "The current would have carried Sarah right to that island."

Captain Murphy saw no point in sharing his sad opinion on where the ocean had taken Sarah. Seeing the pirate ship fleeing the harbor, he offered his telescope to Lord Tufts. "M'Lord, they look to be slipping away."

"We shall deal with them later," said Lord Tufts.

Captain Murphy tried to be delicate. "I'm hoping for the best, sir, I really am, but them seas has been dreadful rough."

"They're calmer now," said Lord Tufts firmly. "We'll find her . . . we'll find my Sarah."

⚓

As the *London Gorilla* distanced itself from the island, Bear paced the deck behind his captain. Black Tooth's anger spewed forth in fits and starts. "How'm I to know royalty is off limits?" he snarled. "Am I some bloomin' mind reader? Kings and queens don't wear signs. Much easier just to kill 'em all."

Regrettably, Bear was double-checking his musket when Black Tooth wheeled around and slammed into him. "You imbecile," hollered Black Tooth, grabbing Bear's left ear and twisting it. "What was you thinking, you half-wit? What you got to say for yourself now, you buffoon? How about dusting off that brain of yours?"

"Sorry, Cap'n, real sorry," said Bear, falling to his knees free of Black Tooth's grip. "Won't happen again." Not liking the look in Black Tooth's eye, he clapped his hands over both his ears.

Black Tooth hollered to Stinger in the crow's-nest. "OY, IS THAT ROYAL PAIN STILL DOGGIN' US?"

"CAN'T TELL YET," Stinger shouted down. "IT'S TOO FOGGY."

"Shoot him," snapped Black Tooth.

"Do what?" asked Bear.

"What good's a lookout that don't look?" said Black Tooth. "Shoot him."

"But, Cap'n, I can't shoot me own mate."

"Well, I can," said Black Tooth, snatching Bear's musket and taking aim at the crow's-nest. "I don't need some useless donkey climbing round me sail tops."

Stinger's head popped over the side of the crow's-nest, and he triumphantly announced, "THE COAST IS CLEAR."

BANG!

The musket ball zinged past Stinger's scalp, and he screamed. "I SAID ALL CLEAR!"

"Should've said so in the first place," muttered Black Tooth as he tossed the musket to Bear and marched away.

⚓

Back at Coal Island, Sarah agonized over her floundering escape plan as she bobbed up and down in the rowboat. Her biggest problem was being too small to use both oars. Sarah wrestled with one oar, but couldn't reach the other. Traveling in circles under the pier meant little chance of leaving the island. Changing her strategy, Sarah held the right oar with both hands and squirmed to hook the left oar with her outstretched foot.

The rowboat crunched into one of the pier's support timbers, and Sarah landed with a *thud* on the bottom of the boat. She lay motionless, straining to hear Nigel above the two dogs' frenzied barking.

"Somebody spot a catfish?" Nigel asked the mangy animals. "Well, how 'bout shutting your biscuit holes and simmering down?"

Floating beneath the pier, Sarah could see the dogs' gleaming yellow eyes as they pressed their snouts between the planks. The animals paused from barking to catch their breath, and Sarah heard their toenails digging into the pier as they fought their leashes.

She silently mouthed, "Nice doggies, good doggies," but the doggies were not swayed. Their barking grew even louder.

"This ain't no way to greet royalty," said Nigel, tugging at the dogs' leashes. "You mutts best make yourselves scarce."

"Serpents in saucepans!" gasped Sarah as Nigel unclipped the first dog's collar.

Sarah jumped from her rowboat and struggled through

waist-deep water for shore. Looking over her shoulder, she saw the first dog burst from the pier.

Sarah's foot hit dry land as the second mutt splashed into the sea and joined its dog-paddling partner. The dogs stopped barking to save their strength for swimming, and Sarah raced into the abandoned shantytown. Even at a full run, she marveled at how the neglected shacks still hung together. Vines choked slanted walls, and moss smothered sagging roofs.

The cramped alleys between the shacks appeared to have been designed by a drunken sailor. An alley never ran straight for more than twenty feet before twisting or turning or stopping for no apparent reason. Darting through the maze, Sarah dodged a one-wheeled cart, a three-legged chair, and a trail of other household goods that had been judged too useless or too heavy by the departing villagers. Even an old piano was plunked in Sarah's path.

The dogs once again found their voices, and Sarah knew their excited yapping meant they had reached land and picked up her scent. Scurrying into a musty shack, Sarah wildly searched for a place to hide but found only four walls and half a roof. She would be caught as soon as the dogs hurtled through the hole where the front door used to be.

Sarah raced from the shack as the frantic barking grew closer. Skidding through mud, she shot out her arms to right herself before missing a washtub and whipping around the next corner. The alley turned sharply back on itself, and Sarah heard the dogs splash through the same mud. She ignored the burning in her legs as she sprinted around another corner.

"Elephants in eggcups!"

A six-foot wooden fence blocked her escape. The dogs would find her at any moment. She quickly looked around and saw an empty rum barrel. Tipping it over, she rolled it to the bottom of the fence. Then, scrambling onto the barrel, Sarah boosted herself over the fence and dropped to the ground.

She pressed her ear to the fence and heard nothing louder than her pounding heart.

CRAAACK!

A dog crashed through the fence.

WHIZZZZ!

The other dog flew past so close that its wet fur brushed Sarah's ear. She backtracked through the new hole in the fence as the dogs skidded to a halt on the other side.

Dashing through the winding alley, Sarah bounced off the washtub and skimmed over the slick mud. Looking behind her, she let out a cry as the dogs flew past the washtub and ripped through the mud. Like two wild beasts, their eyes lost all mercy, their fangs dripped spit, their jaws opened—

"Whooooa!"

Hands jerked Sarah into the air and flipped her upside down.

She swung above snapping jaws, wild eyes, and wrinkled trousers. Blood rushed to her head, and she fought the urge to shriek as saliva seemed to drip upwards from yellowed fangs. Sarah recognized her scowling rescuer even though he was without his wheelbarrow.

"AHHH!"

A wet dog nose punched Sarah's ear.

"You mongrels is too slow," said Mr. Grim. "Get back to the pier."

The panting dogs remained licking their chops inches below Sarah.

"NOW," bellowed Mr. Grim, and the animals skulked away.

"Thank you, sir," said Sarah. "That was very kind of you." Mr. Grim slipped her under his arm and carried her like a loaf of bread. "I said, that was very kind of you," she reminded him. "I'm extremely grateful."

Indeed, Sarah felt ungrateful for noticing that her rescuer stank of fish guts and stale rum. Every time she inhaled, she almost gagged. Every time Mr. Grim inhaled, he sucked air between two rows of shiny reptile teeth. They might have been crocodile or alligator teeth; Sarah couldn't remember the difference, but they were much too pointy to be human teeth.

"It appears safe to set me down now," said Sarah. "No sense tiring yourself out."

Mr. Grim only grunted and kept moving.

"Excuse me, sir," Sarah said a little louder. "But I'm quite capable of walking."

Mr. Grim continued to march and breathe through his open mouth.

"Sir, I insist that you put me down," said Sarah sternly. "I demand it. This is no way to treat a visitor."

"Visitor!" laughed Mr. Grim. "There's a good one."

"Well, I'm afraid I find no humor in uncivilized behavior," said Sarah, realizing at that moment how much she sounded like Aunt Margaret.

"Quit your sniveling."

"I am not sniveling," said Sarah. "I'm asking for a little common courtesy."

Mr. Grim glared straight ahead and tramped through the shantytown. Seeing no benefit in more conversation, Sarah wriggled, but Mr. Grim simply wedged her tighter under his arm. Left with no other choice, Sarah imitated the crab's earlier welcome and sank her teeth into Mr. Grim's finger.

"YEOOOOOW!"

Sarah dropped to the ground as the red-faced man hopped and hollered and waved his hand.

"GET BACK HERE, YOU LITTLE DEVIL!" roared Mr. Grim, but Sarah never slowed as she skidded around a corner and sprinted along a narrow alley.

INSIDE A RAINBOW

SARAH TORE through the shantytown as she spit the foul taste of Mr. Grim's finger from her mouth. While wondering why anyone would ever become a cannibal, she swung around a corner and ran into another dead end. This time a colossal brick wall blocked her path.

"Hello, little girl," Mr. Grim's mocking singsong voice beckoned from another alley. "Come out, come out, wherever you are."

A heavy iron door in the brick wall appeared to be Sarah's only route forward. She tugged and tugged at the handle, but the door wouldn't budge.

"I will find you," promised Mr. Grim, his voice growling from a nearby alley. "And I will beat the tar out of you."

Sarah dropped her shoulder and rammed the iron door. Rebounding hard, she flopped to the ground. Her shoulder stung as she brushed a cloud of dirt from her face.

"Then I'll reacquaint you with them dogs," continued Mr. Grim. "You remember your good friends, don't you, Missy?"

He sounded closer. Sarah picked herself up and rubbed her aching shoulder.

Mr. Grim's voice filled with rage. "AND THEM NO-GOOD MONGRELS WILL CHEW YOUR FACE OFF!"

Desperately, Sarah retreated several steps and breathed deeply. Hurtling forward at full speed, she jumped in the air and hit the door feetfirst.

Bam!

Sarah tumbled inside, and the door slammed shut behind her. She lay stunned for a moment, then springing to her feet, she rubbed her eyes and forgot to close her mouth as she spun in a slow circle.

"Peacocks in parlors!"

She was standing in an enormous room that exploded with color. The floor's ankle-deep carpet cuddled her raw feet in reds and blues and greens and yellows and colors that Sarah had never even seen before. The same bright wool sprouted from the walls and climbed all the way to the frosted glass ceiling fifty feet above. The frosted glass allowed no view of the grayness outside, but it did light the room with a warm glow. Everywhere Sarah looked, mountains of yarn rose to the ceiling. She guessed there had to be over thirty different stacks of purple alone. Mauve, lavender, and lilac yarn towered directly above her.

"I've jumped inside a rainbow!" said Sarah, and surrounded by the glorious, shimmering hues, she became conscious of her dull, grubby blouse and pantalets.

Hearing faint humming, Sarah remembered Mr. Grim and turned for the door. Panic. The door was gone, or at least the shaggy walls did an excellent job of camouflaging it. She scrambled behind a mound of butterscotch yarn and longed for the power to shrink.

As the pleasant humming approached, Sarah cautiously peered around the yarn to spy a small boy no more than five years old, dressed head to toe in a fuzzy whitest-white garment. The one-piece suit with attached slippers and hood allowed only the boy's face to peek out; it was a shiny friendly face covered in freckles.

The boy seemed to be practicing a dance step as he hummed, hopped, and twirled among the yarn. Hop-hop-twirl . . . hop-hop-twirl . . . hop-hop-twirl. He stopped at a pile of fiery red yarn and gathered an armful before hop-hop-twirling away.

Sarah hurried the other way around the red pile, and after two more hops, the boy finished his twirl right in front of her.

"Ahhhhhhhhhhhhh!"

The boy threw up his arms and stood screaming beneath a shower of red yarn.

"I'm sorry," said Sarah. "I didn't mean to startle you." She smiled and offered her hand. "I'm Sarah Tufts, and you are?" The boy only stared as if she were a talking toad. Sarah's half of the handshake hung in the air.

"Yes, I'm afraid I'm in need of a good wash," she said, retrieving her hand and trying a bigger smile. "But I promise I'm perfectly harmless—"

"Amessofbloodyfreckles," blurted the child.

"I beg your pardon," said Sarah, not sure if the small boy had spoken a foreign language.

"A mess of bloody freckles," the boy repeated a little slower. "That's my name. A mess of bloody freckles."

"And what a splendidly unusual name," said Sarah as sincerely as she could muster. True, his freckles numbered more than the stars on a clear night, but Sarah wasn't impressed by the imagination of whoever had named the child.

"Mostly they call me Freck," he said.

"I'm very pleased to meet you, Freck," said Sarah. "And I'm very sorry for barging in like this, but out there is a frightful—" Sarah couldn't understand why Freck's eyes grew wider and wider. He appeared terrified and amazed at the same time.

"Are you quite all right?" she asked him.

"You've been . . ." Freck's whisper trailed off, and he nodded towards the shaggy wall.

"Excuse me?" said Sarah.

"You've been in the . . . ?" Again, Freck's voice dwindled to silence.

"I've been where?" asked Sarah.

"You've been in the . . . Beyond?" Freck shuddered at the sound of the word.

"And didn't enjoy it one bit," said Sarah. "Have you seen the monstrous beasts that run wild out there?"

"Of course not," said Freck. "If I went into the Beyond, I'd die."

"Die?"

"Honest-honest," said Freck. "Everyone knows what happens to two-leggers in the Beyond."

"Two-leggers?"

"Things like you and me, things with two legs," said Freck. "It's the same-same for any two-legger stepping into the Beyond— we ends up the worstest. But don't fret, everything's cheeks high."

"Cheeks high?"

"You know, corners up."

"Excuse me?"

"I'm saying you can show your chewers," said Freck, smiling

to demonstrate what he meant. "'Cuz you'll be cozy-snug in Woolie World."

"Woolie World? What kind of world is this?" said Sarah. "You're all shut in—you can't even see the sun in the sky."

Freck's head tilted like a bewildered puppy. "The sun is right there," he said, pointing to a pile of yellow yarn. "And the sky is over there with the rest of the blues—between blueberry and bruise."

"I don't mean colored wool," explained Sarah. "I mean blue like the real sky and the air you breathe."

"You breathe blue air?" asked Freck.

"Oh, see for yourself," said Sarah, slightly exasperated.

Sarah felt Freck's eyes on her as she rubbed her hands over the wall's yarn camouflage and found an edge of the secret door she had tumbled through. She pried the door open enough for the tips of her fingers to slip into the gap. "Would you mind lending a hand?" Sarah asked the unblinking boy. "My shoulder is still a bit tender."

Freck's feet tiptoed forward while his body leaned backward.

"Perhaps the hinges are rusted shut," said Sarah, trying to ignore the door pinching her fingernails. "I'd say a thorough oiling is in order."

Freck wedged his smaller fingers farther into the narrow opening. "It's cold," he reported.

"Metal always feels cooler," explained Sarah. "Let's pull together on the count of three."

"And it's swishy," said Freck, beginning to squirm.

"Swishy?"

"It confuses my skin." Freck giggled.

"Excuse me?" Sarah pressed her face to the crack and squinted against the rush of air. A whoosh of slobbering pink licked Freck's fingers, and Sarah stared into a dog's yellow eyeball.

Grrrrrrrrrrrrr!

"Vultures in vases!"

A duet of furious barking shot Freck into reverse, and the door pinned Sarah's fingertips. The shrieking boy yanked on Sarah's muddy feet, and she popped free as the door slammed shut, muffling the yapping and scratching.

"It's true!" gasped Freck, bouncing to his feet. "It's honest-honest true!"

"Wait, Freck, please," Sarah urged the child as he scooped up his red yarn. "It's just very unfortunate timing—terrible timing. I believe those two are usually on leashes."

But Freck ran as if his slippers were on fire, and Sarah stood alone.

PULLING STRINGS

FRECK RUSHED through a set of double doors, carrying his load of red yarn. An explosion of colorful wool also coated the floor and walls of this massive room. Freck bounced on tiptoes as he scanned above the hundred chattering children who flitted about in identical white Woolie suits. Quickly he found the boy he wanted. Thomas, the oldest Woolie at twelve, stood a head taller than everyone else.

Freck weaved through the happy crowd towards Thomas, who was helping a three-year-old count backward from ten. Freck could see Thomas peeling and unpeeling his fingers as the tiny Woolie nodded his head in time.

"If a strange two-legger is lurking about the storeroom," Freck said to himself, "Thomas will want to know." Freck dropped to his hands and knees to avoid several Woolies somersaulting through the air and kept crawling towards his target. "And if a strange two-legger is wandering about the Beyond, Thomas will want to know." Freck popped to his feet and bumped through a group of whirling six-year-olds playing tag. "And if a strange two-legger is breathing blue sky, well, surely Thomas will want to know."

Freck leapt to the left, but it was too late. Another Woolie tagged Freck's elbow, and Freck became It. He chased a cluster of girls that scattered in all directions. Another boy zigged and zagged clear of Freck's reach until Freck guessed the boy's next zig and dove at the Woolie's running legs. Freck tagged the boy's ankle before bouncing off the carpet. Again, Freck hopped on his tiptoes to find Thomas. His next hop was a half turn, and he hurried towards Thomas as the game of tag continued behind him.

But Freck's feet slowed as he neared his destination. "And if?" he wondered. "And if the strange two-legger wasn't honest-honest real? Will Thomas want to know that, too? Or will Thomas just think I'm watching the backs of my eyelids again?" After all, thought Freck, he had never before met a girl like Sarah.

"Freck?" Thomas's counting lesson was over. "Freck, is everything cheeks high?"

Freck hesitated.

"We've been waiting on your string," continued Thomas,

and when Thomas put two of his counting fingers between his teeth, Freck knew that any talking would have to wait.

"WSSSSSSSSSSSSSSTTTTTTTTT!"

The piercing whistle transformed every Woolie into a statue. Freck tightened the grip on his red yarn as Thomas slowly raised his arms towards the frosted glass ceiling.

CLAP! CLAP! CLAP!

Thomas's clapping sent frantic Woolies scrambling every-where. Freck hustled to dump his red yarn in its proper place and squeezed back through waves of white Woolie suits to stand next to Thomas. Thomas's next three claps stopped the commo-tion. Woolies stood shoulder to shoulder forming four sides of a gigantic square. At each child's feet lay fluffy mounds of yarn, and Freck spotted his armful of fiery red across the square.

"Every Woolie got their feet on the flat?" Thomas asked. Freck joined everyone in two enthusiastic foot stomps.

"Then all you Tweeners shorten up," said Thomas. "Undies bend your kneelers, and Toppers find your bounce."

The Tweeners crouched, the Undies fell to their knees, and the Toppers hopped in place. The three groups eagerly grabbed string from the piles of yarn. As a Loose-Ender, Freck knew his job meant staying at the edge.

"It's time," announced Thomas. "Follow your bellybuttons!"

Woolies burst across the room, their cheers vibrating through

Freck's chest. The square billowed into a sea of color as children zipped back and forth pulling their yarn. The Undies crawled on knees and elbows, braiding long strands of yarn into the mishmash of wool above them. The Toppers turned backflips and somersaults as they twisted their strands into the growing heaps below. Freck ducked when a Woolie sailed overhead, and heard himself "ooh and aah" when Toppers bounced on the spongy yarn and hovered in midair. The Tweeners crouch-walked through the wool as they pulled their strands behind them. Freck knew it was harder than it looked for Tweeners to keep their yarn above the Undies and below the Toppers.

While plucking the loose end from the nearest mound of silly-sigh pink, Freck joined in the Woolies' song:

> *Pull the string from morn till night,*
> *Hop hop twirl and turn to the right.*
> *Pull the string till your tongue wags red,*
> *Hop hop twirl and go left instead.*
> *Pull the string with a finger and thumb,*
> *Hop hop twirl but keep off your bum.*

Freck laughed as Tweeners leapfrogged each other, but he had to be quick when he handed the pink string to a Topper cartwheeling past.

Pull the string the whole lovely day,
Hop hop twirl and go the other way.
Pull the string till the color grows,
Hop hop twirl and wiggle your nose.
Pull the string while on your belly,
Hop hop twirl but don't get smelly.

Freck had just bent over to give an Undie the loose end of some empty-bowl brown, when a Tweener stumbled into the pile of hiccup blue.

"You're doing wonderful," Thomas advised the little girl as he helped her to her feet. "Just think lighter thoughts."

"Lighter thoughts, lighter thoughts," chanted the girl as she tucked her big-yawn yellow hair back under her Woolie hood. Freck handed her the end of the hiccup blue and watched her hop hop twirl away.

Pull the string till your face is blue,
Hop hop twirl and go someplace new.
Pull the string till you got no hair,
Hop hop twirl and fly over there.
Pull the string till your eyelids droop,
Hop hop twirl but don't miss a loop.

Freck passed a Topper a string of sky blue, and a tingling traveled across the back of his neck.

"Thomas," Freck started, "have you ever seen the sky?"

"You just gave it away," said Thomas, pointing to the somersaulting Topper with the strand of blue yarn.

"But, well, have you seen any other sky?"

"There's a whole pile of it in the storeroom," said Thomas. "You sure nothing is corners down?"

"I mean, is there another kind of sky blue?" asked Freck.

"Another kind of sky blue?" repeated Thomas. "Sky blue is sky blue. What else could it be?"

"That's what I thought," said Freck, and he began to hum along with the string song.

"Bend your kneelers, Freck," said Thomas as he handed Freck a strand of slow-day yellow yarn. "We could use another Undie."

Wondering how Thomas kept track of things, Freck took the yellow strand and joined several Woolies crawling beneath the heaps of wool. On every fourth beat, Freck traded his strand of yarn with the Woolie on his left. On every eighth beat, he traded his strand with the Woolie on his right. Freck carefully avoided the Toppers and Tweeners hop-hop-twirling their way across the yarn.

Pull the string up under and in between,

Hop hop twirl from the place you've been.

Pull the string till you reach the end,

Hop hop twirl and go round the bend.

Pull the string with grasshopper jumps,

Hop hop twirl all around the lumps—

"SHUT UP WITH THAT INFERNAL RACKET!"

The singing evaporated as all around Freck petrified Woolies fell silent. A Topper plopped to the ground beside him. All movement stopped, and Freck got that tummy feeling as if his innards were playing tag.

"I said dummy up," growled Mr. Grim, blustering across the room. "I said nothing about standing around scratching your arses."

Freck kept his eyes low and held his tummy in both hands.

"Don't make me ask twice."

Like every other Woolie, Freck stayed perfectly still, feet flat on the ground.

"GET TO WORK!" roared Mr. Grim.

Freck trembled in place as Thomas cautiously answered. "Master Grim, sir, we can't."

Freck didn't know anyone braver than Thomas.

Mr. Grim threw up his hands. "I don't see why you always gotta be singing them blasted songs."

"Sir, it's how we keep time and find our loops," explained Thomas. "We'll be done in a moment. The depth is almost four-fifths the total area when you multiply by the radius—"

"Shut up with your arithmetic rubbish," snapped Mr. Grim. "Just finish the thing before I knock out four-fifths of your teeth."

Freck stood motionless with the rest of the Woolies, but when Mr. Grim stared right at him, Freck felt his tummy begin a journey up to his chewers.

"Oh, go on," moaned Mr. Grim. "Make your noise."

The Woolies burst into song, and Freck's tummy dropped to its proper place as he dropped to his kneelers and began crawling through the string:

> *Pull the string like two-legger folk,*
> *Hop hop twirl till your legs feel broke.*
> *Pull the string playing hide-and-seek,*
> *Hop hop twirl till your insides leak.*
> *Pull the string like a bullfrog toad,*
> *Hop hop twirl but stay out of my road.*

At Thomas's signal, Freck excitedly took his place on the edge of the square. He picked out several string ends as all around him Undies, Toppers, Tweeners, and Loose-Enders gathered ends from the confusion of yarn.

"Feet on the flat?" asked Thomas.

Freck bobbed his head up and down. How does Thomas always know when it's ready? he thought. All Freck ever saw was a jumble of colors.

"Ten . . . nine . . ." Freck joined in Thomas's countdown. "Eight . . . seven . . . six . . ." All around him Woolies chanted together. Freck gently tugged his loose strands. "Five . . . four . . . three . . ." The mound of yarn slowly tightened. "Two . . . ONE!"

Holding his breath, Freck gave a final pull, and the riot of color magically blossomed into a rug—a dazzling flowering garden of lilies and pansies and daffodils and snapdragons and chrysanthemums and a thousand other brilliant blooms. The rug looked so alive that Freck half expected the ladybug on the rose petal to flap its orange wings and fly away. He carefully stuck out a finger to nudge the ladybug and giggled at the familiar touch of string.

"Stand back. Get back," growled Mr. Grim as he swatted Woolies from his path. He pulled scissors from his pocket and snipped a few stray strings on the rug's fringe. "Out of my way 'less you want to lose a toe."

Mr. Grim stopped to inspect a tiny patch of fiery red. His beady eyes began to twitch, and he finally erupted, "Who's the rattlebrained idjit getting dirt on my new rug?" The Woolies next to Freck quaked in their booties as Mr. Grim leaned into their small faces. "You heard me. Which of you monkeys got the filthy paws?"

Freck remembered tugging on Sarah's muddy feet, and his lips quivered, but words seemed too frightened to leave his throat.

"Fine, I'll string up the whole lot of you—"

"It was me," squeaked Freck.

"You know better than to mess with four-leggers before handling my rugs," said Mr. Grim, poking his finger into a freckle on Freck's forehead.

"Master Grim, sir," stammered Freck, "I wasn't near the four-leggers."

"Don't lie to me, boy," said Mr. Grim, stabbing another freckle. "Where else you gonna find dirt?"

"Maybe it's from . . ." Freck's voice trailed off.

"Maybe it's from what?"

"Maybe it's from . . ." The other Woolies tilted forward to hear Freck's next words, but he still couldn't find his nerve.

"FROM WHERE?" hollered Mr. Grim.

"The Beyond," said Freck.

The other Woolies gasped, and even Mr. Grim took a step back. Freck immediately wished he could change his answer.

"Can I believe my own ears?" said Mr. Grim.

"Master Grim, I didn't mean to," said Freck, fumbling to explain. "I mean, I'd never want to be a frown-maker. I'd—"

"What you waiting for?" Mr. Grim asked the other children. "You Woolies know what happens to anyone gossiping about the Beyond."

"I'm sorry, sir," begged Freck. "Full up—you couldn't fit more sorry in me."

"SNAP TO IT!" ordered Mr. Grim. "OR YOU'LL BE JOINING HIM."

Mr. Grim's threat catapulted the Woolies into action. Children rolled up the new rug to reveal a thick shag carpet beneath it. Freck felt his kneelers buckle as Woolies tugged away a section of the carpet to expose bare rock and a twenty-foot square of wooden planks.

"Please, Master Grim," moaned Freck. "My tongue is done wagging."

Several Woolies struggled to lift each plank, uncovering a gaping pit.

"I promise, I promise," Freck stuttered with fear as two Woolies cranked a large winch that unraveled a fat coil of rope. "Never again, Master Grim." The rope traveled up to the frosted glass ceiling, across the rafters through a series of pulleys, and down to where a bamboo cage hung at its end.

The two Woolies lowered the cage, and its door swung on its hinges as the cage stopped level with Freck's feet. He felt Mr. Grim's rough hand between his shoulder blades.

The shove launched Freck's chest forward, and his legs didn't catch up until he crashed into the far side of the bamboo cage. He heard a *click* and spun for the door, but Mr. Grim had already jammed an iron pin into the lock high above Freck's head.

"Please, Master Grim, please," whimpered Freck, and the cage wobbled as he looked down through the bamboo bars at the shimmering pool of bad-apple black water below. He didn't blame the other Woolies for quick-footing back from the pit.

With the same scissors he had used to trim the new rug, Mr. Grim pricked the tip of his own finger and held it over the edge of the pit. A drop of blood fell with a *plop*.

WHAM!

Five scaly no-leggers crashed to the surface and battled for the tiny splash of red.

"It breaks my heart when a Woolie don't obey the rules," said Mr. Grim. "Fool stories about the Beyond. Ha! Everyone knows one step outside them walls and the no-leggers will be feasting on your bottom half."

Freck tried to pry his eyes from the gray shapes slashing through the dark pool. Water twinkled across mouths filled with pointy chewers.

"Still, it's just as well," continued Mr. Grim, "'cuz the poison out there will make your innards explode—and there ain't nothing cozy-snug about that."

Freck gasped as a no-legger surged from the water and chomped at the air. He heard other Woolies squeal and quick-foot even farther back from the pit.

"LOWER THE CAGE," demanded Mr. Grim.

Freck watched the two Woolies blubber tears as they cranked the winch. The cage jerked and slowly sank into the pit, and Freck fought the smooth bamboo bars. His whimpers mixed with the echoes of hungry no-leggers thrashing deep below.

"STOP YOUR WICKEDNESS!" demanded a voice from above. "And free that boy this instant!"

Freck's cage wobbled to a halt, his head and shoulders still above the rim of the pit. The Woolies operating the winch joined the others in staring at the peculiar sight.

"She's real!" sputtered Freck. "She's honest-honest real."

"What the devil?" fumed Mr. Grim as he marched to Sarah.

"How can you treat a child so cruelly?" asked Sarah. "How can you be so nasty? How can you be so evil? How can you be so—"

Freck stood on his toes to watch Mr. Grim clamp a hand over Sarah's mouth.

"Nobody tells me how to run my affairs," roared Mr. Grim.

Freck continued to gawk even after Mr. Grim had hauled Sarah from the room.

"Reverse the crank!" yelled Thomas.

For a moment, Freck had forgotten that he stood locked behind bars, but he grabbed the bamboo as the cage jerked up to floor level. A Topper scrambled onto Thomas's shoulders and popped the iron pin from the lock.

The door swung open, and Freck scurried to solid ground. He dropped onto his bellybutton and hugged the carpet as all around him Woolies burst into a hundred conversations—each one about the girl who had dared to question Master Grim.

Freck rose to his kneelers and announced, "Her name is Sarah."

FAMILY
REUNION

NIGEL TWITCHED and nervously smiled at the search party he escorted along the island's shoreline. Fog blurred the ghostly figures of the *Shy Mermaid*'s crew fanned out across the dreary beach. Nigel fingered his Adam's apple as he walked between Lord Tufts and Captain Murphy.

"We're flattered that royalty would visit our little island," gushed Nigel. "The king's cousin, imagine that. Quite an honor, really it is."

Nigel filled the somber silence by wiping his clammy brow.

"Too bad we didn't know you was coming—a real disgrace it is," Nigel insisted enthusiastically. "We'd of planned a proper welcome."

Nigel picked at his mustache and wondered how long a royal person usually went without talking.

"I was unaware this island even existed," said Captain Murphy.

"It don't really," said Nigel with a poorly timed chuckle. "Coal miners took most of it with them. They deserted the place long ago. Only ones left is a handful of honest folk leading peaceful lives." Nigel avoided Captain Murphy's eyes. "You know, raising a few sheep, spinning a bit of yarn."

"You're a rare one to be knitting booties," said Captain Murphy.

Twenty yards farther along the beach lay the shoe that Sarah had kicked off when she washed ashore on the island. If it weren't so foggy, Lord Tufts would have already spotted the footwear. Luckily, he was heading straight for the single clue that proved his daughter had safely reached land; fifteen more yards and he would step right on the shoe . . . ten more yards . . . five more—

"Your Lordship!" beckoned a crewman. "Over here."

Lord Tufts rushed away, and Sarah's shoe lay undiscovered.

Nigel caught up to Lord Tufts as the white-faced man gathered bits of splintered wood from the wet sand.

"Heaven help her," whispered Lord Tufts.

"I'm afraid them breakers is terribly unfriendly," said Nigel.

"Any footprints have washed away," said Captain Murphy, examining the surrounding sand.

Lord Tufts sank to his knees and clutched a larger shred of the chewed crate. Nigel clearly saw the royal coat of arms stamped on the wood.

"The sea has taken my only daughter," sobbed Lord Tufts.

Nigel had to look away as the man buried his face in his sleeve and wept. Nigel shuffled in place and kicked at the sand. Wretched sea air, he thought as his head rolled back with the unexpected swell of his chest. The damp is surely playing havoc with my windpipe.

As Captain Murphy put a comforting hand on Lord Tufts's shoulder, Nigel scratched his nose to hide a sniffle.

⚓

Sarah lay on the floor of Mr. Grim's office, her wrists and ankles bound by thick purple and lime green yarn. As elsewhere in Woolie World, yarn sprouted from every surface and dripped from the rafters. Sarah flailed and kicked when Mr. Grim stuffed her legs into a large multicolored pouch. Calloused hands squeezed her elbows and muscled the soft pocket of wool up her body and over her shoulders. Wriggling didn't stop Mr. Grim from knotting the pouch's drawstring around her neck.

"You should be ashamed of yourself," said Sarah as Mr. Grim secured a long rope to the pouch. The rope traveled through several pulleys before it disappeared high in the shaggy rafters. "What kind of pitiful coward terrorizes children?"

"Mind your tongue, Missy," said Mr. Grim. "I still ain't decided what's to be done with you." He grunted and hauled on the rope. Sarah's pouch jerked from the floor, and she found herself swinging eye level with the sour man.

"I'm not frightened of ruffians like you," said Sarah, feeling very dishonest.

"Only proves how daft you are," said Mr. Grim, sticking his face into Sarah's.

"Skunks in trunks!" she gasped.

The man's nose hairs fluttered, and Sarah thought the hot stench of his breath would melt her skin.

"He's here!" wheezed an out-of-breath Nigel flying through the door.

"Who's here?" said Mr. Grim.

"The royal rotter from the ship," explained Nigel. "Lord Tufts."

"Father!"

"You're alive?" asked Nigel, seeing Sarah for the first time.

"And you're in trouble," said Sarah, feeling braver just knowing that her father was on the island. "When my father gets through with you, you'll both be sorry."

"Not good, not good," worried Nigel, pulling at his mustache. "He already thinks she's dead."

"But you must tell Father I'm still—"

Sarah tried to spit out the ball of apricot yarn that Mr. Grim jammed in her mouth. The taste of fuzz curled her tongue, and her gibberish turned to muffled panic as he tied the gag in place.

"What do we do?" asked Nigel. "What do we do?"

"Quiet," growled Mr. Grim. "It's not our problem his brat washed up on my shore."

Sarah concentrated on breathing through her nose as Nigel twitched and jittered about the office.

"He wants a word with you, Pa."

"Tell him I'm busy," said Mr. Grim.

"He's royalty."

"I don't give a fiddler's fart," said Mr. Grim. "Get rid of him."

Nigel squirmed and admitted in a whisper that carried clearly to Sarah's ears, "I left Lord Tufts and Captain Murphy waiting in the storeroom."

"YOU NINNY!" exploded Mr. Grim. "Fetch them here before they start snooping about."

Nigel bolted out the door, and Mr. Grim returned to heaving the rope that hoisted Sarah's pouch. She felt herself lurch up and swing into the rafters, where the pouch blended so well with the ceiling's yarn that Sarah knew she was invisible from below. Still, she had a bird's-eye view of Mr. Grim sitting behind his desk.

"You are an awful, awful man," Sarah tried to say, but with enough yarn in her mouth to knit a pair of mittens, her words came out sounding like, "Mmm mmm m mmmm mmmm mmm."

Mr. Grim pulled a pistol from his desk drawer, and Sarah stopped mumbling. "Good," he said, resting the pistol across his lap. "One more peep and you'll be an orphan."

A knock sounded at the door, and the weaselly Nigel popped his head inside. "Sorry to disturb you, Master Grim," said Nigel with a wink. "I hope you're not busy." Nigel winked again. "Lord Tufts and Captain Murphy are here to see you." Nigel winked a third time, and Sarah wanted to poke out his eye.

"Please, please," said Mr. Grim in a saintly voice. "Show the gentlemen in."

Sarah felt a glow of hope as Captain Murphy stepped through the door, but her insides plummeted when her father walked slack-armed and lifeless across the office. Nigel scurried to clear yarn from seats for the men, and Lord Tufts slumped into a chair. Sarah desperately wanted to call out, but she could see Mr. Grim's hand below the desk top and the pistol pointed right at her father.

"Your Lordship, what an honor," said Mr. Grim, stroking his white beard like a frail Father Christmas. "Forgive me for not standing, but my rusty pegs don't work so good."

"Save your strength, sir," said Captain Murphy kindly.

"As a man who knows the joy of fatherhood," said Mr. Grim, "I was heartbroken to hear of your loss."

"Sarah was so like her mother," said Lord Tufts softly, as if talking more to himself than the other men in the room. "Too much an angel for this world."

With no free hands, Sarah could only wipe her tears against her shoulder.

"I shall pray for her soul," said Mr. Grim. "Did you ever have little ones, Captain?"

"None for me," said Captain Murphy. "Never had the time."

"Well, Captain, all sons and daughters are blessed gifts." Mr. Grim paused for a sigh before addressing Sarah's father. "My son Nigel didn't mention the reason for your voyage, My Lordship."

As Sarah waited for her father to respond, her eyes were drawn to Mr. Grim fiddling with the pistol on his lap.

"We're on our way to one of the king's new colonies," explained Captain Murphy. "That is to say, Lord Tufts and his daughter were on board when Sarah, ah, when Sarah was, well, she . . ." Captain Murphy skipped over the tragic details. "Lord Tufts is to be the new governor of the colony."

"The king's representative—very impressive. My congratulations on your posting, Lord Tufts." Mr. Grim smiled, showing his pointy teeth. "I hope it brings some small consolation."

Lord Tufts did not reply, and Sarah watched the other men wait in strained silence. Captain Murphy shifted in his chair, and Nigel nearly rubbed the mustache off his upper lip. Mr. Grim flexed his pistol hand and strummed his beard. Sarah caught the old man using a thumb and forefinger to prop up the corners of his painful smile.

"Your island appears to have been misplaced by the mapmakers," said Captain Murphy at last. "My charts show no sign of it."

"After the coal mines played out, I guess they couldn't be bothered with us," said Mr. Grim. "No need to waste good ink drawing a hollow rock. You see, Captain, everything of value has left this island. If I was any spryer, I'd leave the place myself—not to say I'm valuable." Mr. Grim forced a laugh and followed it with a wet cough.

"Mr. Grim, I'm wiser than you think," said Lord Tufts, suddenly waking from his trance.

"Afraid you've lost me, sir," said Mr. Grim, his eyes no longer matching his smile.

"I know full well what goes on here," said Lord Tufts.

"You do?" asked Mr. Grim.

Mr. Grim's coughing fit shook his body, but Sarah could swear that through the ugly hacking she heard a *click* as he cocked his deadly weapon. Sarah bit hard on her woolen gag as Mr. Grim aimed the hidden pistol directly at Lord Tufts.

FOUR-LEGGERS
AND PUNY-NEWS

FROM HER pouch in the rafters, Sarah wanted to yell and scream and warn her father about Mr. Grim's pistol. But she knew that one mumble from her wool-filled mouth would mean her father's execution. Surely the pistol couldn't miss from such close range, and surely the blast of lead would shred Lord Tufts's heart.

"It's obvious," said Lord Tufts, "that this is where you weave the famous chromatic rugs."

"My Lord, you're too clever," said Mr. Grim, relaxing his trigger finger.

Sarah unclenched her body.

"Famous cro-what?" asked Captain Murphy, confused.

"Chromatic—fancy word for color," Mr. Grim kindly

explained. "But I wouldn't be calling them famous. Shabby old mats, mostly."

"Mr. Grim's modesty doesn't allow him to boast," said Lord Tufts. "Yet every fashionable lady dreams of a chromatic in her front parlor."

"Aye," agreed Mr. Grim. "We've had a couple years of popularity."

"My sister Margaret would trade our cousin's crown for that masterpiece," said Lord Tufts with a wave towards the floor. "I assure you, Captain Murphy, the rug beneath us is priceless."

"Now I understand your desire for secrecy," said Captain Murphy.

"We're sorry to intrude," continued Lord Tufts. "However, I have a favor to ask of you. Mr. Grim, I should like your permission to erect a small monument for my daughter—for Sarah."

Sarah heard her name catch in her father's throat, and she watched the other men look away as Lord Tufts wiped his eyes.

"Something on the beach? That's a fine idea," agreed Mr. Grim. "Nigel will be happy to assist you. Now you must stay and have supper with us."

"Sir, we appreciate the invitation," said Captain Murphy, "but we've pirates to find and justice to be dealt."

"I wish I could help in such a noble deed," said Mr. Grim. "I'm sure you'll give those vermin the lashing they deserve."

"That I shall promise you, sir," said Lord Tufts, rising to shake Mr. Grim's hand.

"Once again, my deepest condolences," said Mr. Grim, feebly returning Lord Tufts's firm grip.

Again, Sarah chomped down on her woolen gag, disappointed that her father had not ripped off the evil man's arm.

"I'll pray your future voyages are safer ones," said Mr. Grim, with another limp handshake for Captain Murphy. "Nigel, please escort these gentlemen to the beach."

"Right this way, sirs," said Nigel, directing the men towards the door.

Sarah felt as if her father's departure sucked the air from the room. Rapid breaths swelled her chest and flared her nostrils. Her eyes began to flood as she fought her screams.

The door swung shut, and Mr. Grim's smile vanished.

"What a daft fool," he said, stashing the pistol in his desk drawer. "Your father appears no brighter than coal dust," he called up to Sarah. Through with acting frail, Mr. Grim huffed his way to the rope that anchored Sarah's pouch in the ceiling. "In fact, that's my opinion of all royalty." He untied the rope and lowered Sarah to the floor. "It don't take half a brain to be king—you need only find yourself born into the correct baby carriage."

Mr. Grim huffed some more and pulled the gag from Sarah's

mouth. The yarn had soaked up all her saliva, and her dry teeth snagged on her parched tongue.

"Cheer up," said Mr. Grim as Sarah spit bits of fuzz and flexed her jaw. "I'll take good care of His Lordship's precious angel. Pretty soon you'll think of me as your new pa."

"I'd sooner die," said Sarah, sniffing back a tear.

"Make trouble and you'll get your wish."

"My father's not through with you—"

"Your father thinks you're dead," hissed Mr. Grim. "Oh, I've no doubt you were the cherry pie on his window sill, but now that he's gone, best you forget him."

Sarah wanted to be brave and not give Mr. Grim the satisfaction of seeing her cry, but as she grit her teeth her watery eyes spilled another tear.

⚓

A short time later, Mr. Grim was tugging Sarah by the hand down a ruby red hallway. The shaggy carpet sprang beneath her feet, and Sarah might have enjoyed the elastic steps if she weren't so preoccupied with her one-piece white Woolie suit. She adjusted the small holes in the hood to line up with her ears. She had already figured out why there was a trapdoor in the rear of the suit. She could undo a few buttons instead of taking off the entire suit if she needed to, well, you know. Sarah had thought the wool would be scratchy, but the white suit felt as soft as a kitten.

"I don't tolerate gossip," said Mr. Grim. "Them others got no need of hearing wild tales about the Beyond."

"You can tie me up and hang me from the ceiling," said Sarah. "But you can't stop me from telling the truth."

"Suit yourself," said Mr. Grim, casually pulling the scissors from his pocket. "Jabber all you want about nonsense outside these walls." He tightened his grip on her hand. "Except then I'll have to snip off one of your fingers." Sarah watched in terror as he snip-snipped the gleaming blades. "More talk—more fingers. YOU GOT ME?"

Speechless, Sarah could only nod. In her mind she saw her thumb lying on the floor and herself no longer able to count past nine.

"Yet if you don't natter like an old hen, you'll be fine," said Mr. Grim, easing his grip enough for the blood to flow back into Sarah's hand. "I feed you, clothe you, and keep the rain off your head. Even a finicky Frenchman would be thanking me."

Mr. Grim yanked Sarah closer as three Woolies rushed by with armloads of sun-yellow yarn. The children disappeared through swinging double doors that leaked music. Sarah recognized the song that Freck had been humming.

Pull the string through valleys and dips,
Hop hop twirl and then lick your lips.

A singing Woolie flew out the doors. When he saw Mr. Grim, the small boy lowered his head and silently raced past, hugging the wall.

Pull the string with eyes wide open,
Hop hop twirl and quit your mopin'.

Mr. Grim plowed into the vast room, pulling Sarah behind him. The swinging door smacked her from behind, but Sarah smiled at the sight of Freck safely singing along with the other Woolies.

Pull the string till the colors fade,
Hop hop twirl and dream of marmalade.

Children scooted across the room, hopping and bending as they added their strands to growing mounds of yarn. More than a hundred colors blended together in the haphazard heaps.

Sarah felt the eyes of every Woolie on her. Children crawling under the wool stopped and stared. Children wading through the wool stopped and stared. Children soaring over the mesh of colors dropped to the floor and stared. By the time Mr. Grim had towed her to where Freck stood with his mouth open, the entire room was quietly watching.

"Put her to work in the nursery," growled Mr. Grim, throwing Sarah at Freck's feet.

"Yes, Master Grim," Freck quickly agreed as he helped Sarah up.

"Maybe you can stay out of the pit if you train her proper," said Mr. Grim. "So none of your frown-maker habits."

"None, Master Grim, honest-honest," said Freck, stretching the sleeve of Sarah's Woolie suit as he rushed her away through the silent crowd.

"DON'T STAND THERE GAWKING," bellowed Mr. Grim. "BACK AT IT, YOU LAZY SLUGS."

The Woolies burst into song and jumped to work, while on the far side of the room Freck finally risked a whisper. "Thank you, Sarah. You saved me from the no-leggers."

"You're welcome, Freck," said Sarah, relaxing more the farther she traveled from Mr. Grim. "Helping one another is what friends do." Sarah truly believed this, but she also knew that she was the one who needed Freck's help now. Sarah sized up Freck while wondering if the rowboat still drifted beneath the pier. She wished that the boy were a little bigger so he could better manage an oar.

Reaching another set of double doors, Freck politely held one open as Sarah stepped into a huge room so white and fluffy that it looked as if a snowstorm had just dumped its load. Pure ivory yarn covered walls and floors so white that they seemed to reflect the glowing light from the frosted glass high above.

"Penguins in pillows!" gasped Sarah. Hundreds of spotless lambs scampered about this wonderland. It took her another half second to pick out the dozens of small children in the room; these two- and three-year-olds were hardly bigger than the lambs, and their white Woolie suits blended with the lambs' white fleece. Some of the Woolies were bathing and grooming the tiny animals. Others fed them from baby bottles.

One Woolie was teaching a newborn lamb to walk by prancing on his own hands and knees. When the boy signaled that it was his student's turn, the lamb stood on four clumsy legs and took a wobbly step . . . another wobbly step . . . and plopped on its backside. Sarah's laughter alerted the other Woolies to her presence, and they waved and smiled.

"What is this place?" asked Sarah, returning the friendly greetings.

"This is the beginning," said Freck, leading Sarah across the room. "Everything begins with the puny-new four-leggers."

"Four-leggers?"

"You know, two more legs than us."

"I guess that's one way of naming things," said Sarah, petting a curious lamb nudging her leg. "So these children really look after an entire room full of four-leggers?"

"Who else would?" asked Freck.

"I'm not sure," said Sarah. "They just seem so young."

"Puny-new Woolies always take care of puny-new four-leggers," explained Freck. "Master Grim says it only makes sense 'cuz they're both puny-new."

Hearing Mr. Grim's name, Sarah refocused on her escape plan. "It'll be easy enough to get outside again," she said. "We can slip out the door—"

"You heard Master Grim," said Freck, stopping dead in his tracks. "You heard what he said about no-leggers and poison out there."

"The air is fine in the Beyond—"

"Shhh," urged Freck, swiveling about to check if anyone had overheard Sarah. "Never ever say that word or we'll both end up the worstest."

"All right, all right—cheeks high, corners up, whatever," said Sarah. "But the air is perfectly safe in the you-know-where."

"You said it was blue."

"Yes, the sky is blue, but—"

"I can't breathe blue air," said Freck, taking Sarah's hand and continuing through the lambs. "And you and me both heard those growling no-leggers."

"Well, actually . . ." But Sarah decided not to correct Freck's leg count. If she wanted Freck to venture outside, why add more monsters to his list of fears? Besides, she reasoned, those two mangy dogs were probably safely back on their leashes. Freck would never again have to worry about them licking the soft hand that Sarah held—a hand so different from Mr. Grim's rough sweaty paws. "Well, actually, I think the only monster we need to worry about is Mr. Grim."

"That's 'cuz you've never been in the pit," said Freck, and his forehead wrinkled at the memory. "The pit is bubbling with no-leggers."

"Those no-leggers are called sharks," said Sarah, tripping over a lamb that scampered between her legs.

"A different name doesn't change who they are," said Freck, helping Sarah to her feet. "It's always the same-same. No-leggers hate Woolies. Master Grim says it's 'cuz they're jealous we got two good legs. Master Grim says no-leggers crawl around on their bellies dreaming of chewing off legs."

"Freck, you should know that there are plenty of well-behaved no-leggers," said Sarah. "Worms and snails and garter snakes are no-leggers, and they'd never hurt a soul. And I can't see beetles being jealous of spiders just because spiders have eight legs."

"*Eight*-leggers?"

"I'm certainly not envious of centipedes and their hundred legs."

"A *hundred-legger?*" marveled Freck.

"They're only teeny-weeny legs," explained Sarah as they reached another set of double doors.

The next room had the usual shaggy walls and frosted glass ceiling, but Sarah thought for a moment that she had stepped outside. A field of lush green grass carpeted the floor. Hundreds and hundreds of ewes wandered freely, munching on this giant lawn. Inside a locked pen, a large ram with curled horns sniffed the air and pawed the ground.

Several Woolies inched along on their knees, carefully arranging individual grass seeds in a patch of fresh earth. More Woolies covered the seeds with a dusting of soil, and other Woolies followed with watering jugs. The happy group welcomed Sarah and Freck.

Sarah wished Aunt Margaret were there, just to see her reaction. If finding a stray crumb on the horsehair sofa caused a furor, planting a meadow in her front parlor would surely send Aunt Margaret into conniptions.

The ram snorted and bumped his pen.

"It's all cheeks high," said Freck, leading her into the room. "Living string don't hurt you, and neither do the four-leggers."

"Doesn't anyone just call them sheep?" said Sarah.

"Sheep?" giggled Freck. "What a silly name."

"What's so silly about sheep?"

"It doesn't tell you anything about who they are."

Sarah couldn't argue with this point and decided against mentioning that some silly people called "living string" grass.

Freck guided her towards a tall boy—the first Woolie she guessed to be older than herself. On the boy's command twelve sheep spun in circles while balancing on their hind legs.

"That's amazing," said Sarah.

"That's Thomas," said Freck. "Four-leggers listen to him."

Thomas glanced at Sarah, but ignored her wave and returned to his sheep. Thomas clapped once, and the twelve sheep organized themselves into one perfectly straight line. He clapped twice, and the sheep arranged themselves into two rows of six. He clapped four times, and the sheep arranged themselves into four rows of three.

An abrupt sound of crunching wood unsettled the sheep, and they shuffled and bobbed their heads. Sarah looked back to see the ram's next head butt rattle his pen.

Thomas snapped his fingers, and the ewes snapped to attention and began springing over each other's backs; the first row hopped over the second row as the third row hopped over the fourth row. Thomas kept snapping his fingers, and the sheep kept sailing over one another. To Sarah it appeared the animals were playing leapfrog.

"I've never seen anything like it," said Sarah.

"It puts more bounce in the string," said Freck.

"Bounce in the string?"

"The string that comes from the four-leggers," said Freck. "If four-leggers learn proper, then the string knows how to act proper."

If Sarah hadn't been so busy wondering whether Thomas could touch both sides of the rowboat at the same time, she would have had some questions about training yarn while it still grew on the sheep.

Sarah heard a crash and clamoring hoofs, and loud gasps from the grass-planters. She turned to see the ram barreling right at her.

WHERE WOOL
COMES FROM

SCREAMING, SARAH turned to run and tumbled over Freck. A few yards away the charging ram lowered his horns, and Sarah covered her eyes.

"WHSSSSSSSTT!"

A piercing whistle tightened her eardrums and then . . . nothing. Sarah peeked between her fingers and saw the ram's snout frozen within inches of her face.

Thomas whistled again, and the ram trotted back to his pen. Unsteadily, Sarah picked herself up from the grass.

"How on earth did you do that?" Sarah asked Thomas.

Freck was the one who answered proudly, "Thomas is the cleverest Woolie in the whole world."

"Get her moving before Master Grim's corners start to

droop," Thomas instructed Freck. His cold tone didn't invite more conversation.

"No tangles, Thomas," said Freck, grabbing Sarah's hand and heading for the door.

"It was nice to meet you, Thomas," said Sarah, but Thomas was already walking away and he didn't bother to look back. "Is he always so short?" asked Sarah.

"Short?" asked Freck. "Thomas is the tallest Woolie in the whole world."

"I mean short like blunt," said Sarah. "Short like rude."

"Thomas is usually wonderful-wonderful," said Freck as they reached another set of doors. "He must have a lot on his brain today."

The next room was full of sheep with such ridiculously overgrown coats that they looked like gigantic balls of wool. Sarah only knew which way a sheep was facing because the tails wagged side to side and the mouths chewed in circles. How boring, she thought, to spend every day eating grass and growing your hair. She found herself remembering some of the girls at her old school. Always worried about how long their hair was, and how shiny their hair was, and how curly their hair was. Those girls would have been happy sheep.

"Watch your step," warned Freck, and Sarah skipped aside to avoid some sheep droppings. Another way Sarah learned to distinguish between the sheep's two fluffy ends was that nice green grass entered at the front, while something neither nice nor green exited at the rear.

Two Woolies arrived to sweep up the droppings and deposit them on a conveyor belt that traveled the length of the room and disappeared through a hole in the far wall.

Woolies herded the bushy sheep in single file along a path of colorful tiles that led into a tube four feet high and twenty feet long. Hoofs clicked and clattered on the tile as each sheep squeezed into the tube. Sarah heard buzzing and whizzing and a few bleats, and then . . . a bald, wrinkly sheep exited from the other end of the tube. Woolies dressed the skinny sheep in bright knit suits that looked like Woolie suits with two extra legs. However, the sheep seemed only concerned with getting a mouthful of grass.

A flurry of fresh-cut wool blinded Sarah as she stepped into the next room. The light fleece was heavy with the oily scent of sheep. She felt Freck's hand leading her as the raw wool rained from the shearing tube that poked through the wall.

"This is where the string-to-be comes next," explained Freck, pulling her clear of the fleece. But Sarah was only listening to the music that floated to her ears.

"Songbirds and cinnamon!" she gasped softly. "Have you ever heard such sweetness?"

"They're making string."

"Shhh," whispered Sarah, not wanting to miss one note of the magical tune.

An army of Woolies pedaled row upon row of what looked like wooden carriage wheels strung together. Woolies perched atop the wheels pumped their legs while other Woolies fed clumps of raw wool into the gyrating contraptions. The wheels transformed coarse fleece into fine strands of creamy yarn. Sarah's head spun in happy circles as she followed the hypnotic wheels whose whirring spokes plinked out the enchanting melody.

A string of yarn from each wheel traveled overhead through pulleys and exited the room through penny-sized holes in the far wall. Sarah was still marveling at the spinning music when Freck led her through another set of doors.

In the dyeing room, the strings of yarn traveled from the ceiling and split into a complex web that fed dozens of huge wooden vats. Each vat contained a Woolie submerged up to his or her chin in the colored dye. Moving like human butter churners, the Woolies splashed about to ensure that the natural-colored yarn absorbed the dye.

"Those poor children float about the entire day?" asked Sarah.

"Color bugs gotta kick up the color so it sticks to the string," explained Freck.

"String hardly seems worth drowning for," said Sarah, noticing a Woolie dog-paddling in blue dye.

Freck must have followed her gaze because just then he asked, "Is there honest-honest another blue sky?"

"Besides the blue sky on the other side of that glass?" said Sarah, nodding towards the ceiling.

"Glass?" said Freck. "Oh, you mean the top of the world."

Sarah didn't know where to begin, but she knew that she had a lot of explaining ahead of her.

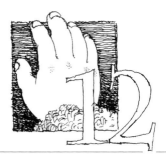

WHERE BABIES
COME FROM

NIGEL TIMIDLY entered his father's office. "Can I have a word, Pa?"

Mr. Grim was inspecting a green woolen potholder decorated with a delicate design of twigs and blueberry clusters.

"Look at this," grumbled Mr. Grim, tossing the potholder to Nigel. "It's the handiwork of some puny-new."

"Bleeding good for a first-timer," said Nigel, admiring the flawless work of art. He rubbed the soft wool against his cheek. "Bleeding bloody good."

"Who asked you?" said Mr. Grim, snatching the potholder and resuming his search for defects. "It needs a tighter weave."

"A tighter weave?" said Nigel.

"I want it so you can't fit a fart between them stitches," said

Mr. Grim. "And chatting with the new brat got me thinking—slice off fingers and they got smaller hands. Smaller hands get into smaller spaces, and smaller spaces means a tighter weave. It's a brilliant idea, don't you think?"

"Cutting off their fingers?" said Nigel.

"Not all of them," said Mr. Grim. "Don't be daft. I'm talking about snipping off a couple lousy fingers from each hand. Baby fingers is useless anyway, and lazy fingers only get in the road."

"Lazy fingers?" said Nigel.

"You know, them ones," said Mr. Grim, trying to extend his fourth finger, but having no success separating it from his index and little finger. "See, the ruddy thing just follows them others—lazy finger's got no mind of its own."

"I think it's called the 'ring' finger," said Nigel.

"I don't give a flying fig," said Mr. Grim. "And what you doing here anyways?"

Nigel scratched his shoulder and tweaked his mustache. "I need someone helping me outside."

"Woolies in the Beyond?" said Mr. Grim. "You sick in the head?"

"The new girl's already been in the Beyond. No harm if she sees it again," reasoned Nigel. "And an extra hand outside would make things easier."

"For you," said Mr. Grim.

"I'd still do my share of—"

"Quit your bellyaching," growled Mr. Grim, and he returned to studying the potholder.

Since a desk stood between him and an ear twisting, Nigel felt brave enough to continue, "I'm just thinking how the new girl's so feisty and a bit of tough slogging might slow her down. And, well, if she lent a hand outside, then I could tend to more things inside and free up more time for you—more time you could spend in the nursery." Nigel wanted to appear calm, but he could feel his Adam's apple bobbing up and down his thin neck.

Mr. Grim threw down the potholder. "Them shameful mutts couldn't catch a cold."

"What?" said Nigel, confused.

"They should've given the new girl a good ravaging," said Mr. Grim. "But nothing works hard when its belly is full."

"I gotta feed them," said Nigel.

"They got teeth. Let them find their own supper," said Mr. Grim. "I imagine rats is plenty tasty when you got nothing else."

Defeated, Nigel headed to the door. "I'll empty their bowls."

"Good," said Mr. Grim. "Oh, and one more thing, take the new girl outside and have her tidy up the pile."

"That's what I just got done bloody telling you," said Nigel, turning around.

"So now you're giving the orders?"

"It was a suggestion."

"But it was all your notion, was it?" asked Mr. Grim.

"Well . . . ," hummed Nigel, suspicious of where his pa's questions led.

"You cooked up the whole plan on your own?" Mr. Grim wondered aloud. "Such a big brain shouldn't need anyone else's help outside."

Nigel felt his pa eyeballing him, and he knew the prudent answer was a humble one. "Pa, it's another of your brilliant ideas."

⚓

Back in the color room, Sarah watched several Woolies use tall bamboo pitchforks to pull the wet yarn from the dye vats. The children twisted the yarn around the pitchforks as if stealing spaghetti from a giant's bowl—except that this giant liked turtle green and canary yellow and squirrel gray spaghetti. The Woolies untwisted their pitchforks to drape the dripping yarn on clotheslines to dry.

Below the clotheslines, a group of Woolies played tag, and the yarn fluttered in their breeze. "It's nice to see that not every Woolie is slaving away at some job," said Sarah.

"Flitting 'neath the string *is* their job," explained Freck. "They keep the world moving so the string dries faster."

"Doesn't anyone ever get to play?" asked Sarah.

"What's play?"

"Play is when you do things just for fun," said Sarah. "When you do things that make you feel good."

"Then I'm full up with play," said Freck. "Singing in the weave makes me feel good, flitting 'neath the string makes me feel good, and tending to puny-news makes me feel good."

"It isn't play if Mr. Grim forces you to do it," said Sarah as she watched the Woolies collect dry yarn off the clotheslines. The Woolies wound the long strands around their bodies—head to toe like human spools—and hopped from the room. "At least, it doesn't seem as if it should be. Perhaps you just think you're having fun."

"Isn't that enough?" asked Freck.

"I'm not sure," Sarah admitted, and she rethought her definition of play as they left the room and strolled along the hallways. "Play," decided Sarah, "is the other fun things you want to do when Mr. Grim isn't bossing you about."

"But what else should I want to do?" asked Freck.

"There are plenty of things to do in the Beyo—" Sarah quickly corrected herself as they entered the nursery. "I mean to say, there are plenty of things to do outside."

The nursery was bright and shaggy like every other room in Woolie World. Sarah and Freck walked among the youngest Woolies, who crawled and tottered on the soft carpet. Older

Woolies fed, bathed, and dressed the cheery toddlers. "There are so many of them," said Sarah. "And they're so young. Where did they all come from?"

"Puny-news come from the same place as you and me," said Freck. "They come from cocoons."

"Cocoons?"

"Cocoons grew three more puny-news this morning," said Freck, pointing to where three babies hung snug and happy inside woolen pouches suspended from the ceiling. Sarah recognized the woolen pouches as smaller versions of the pouch Mr. Grim had used to hang her from the rafters.

"Babies—puny-news—don't magically appear," said Sarah.

"Sure they do," said Freck. "Those cocoons were empty before the long blink."

"I beg your pardon?"

"The long blink," said Freck. "When you set down your head and close your lids."

"Oh, you mean, sleep."

"Sleep?" repeated Freck. "You've got a word for everything."

"It might seem so," said Sarah. "But I've no word for babies mysteriously popping up at breakfast."

"GET OVER HERE, GIRL!"

The commandment was a high-pitched whine, and Sarah turned to see Nigel by the door, scratching his mustache.

"My name is Miss Sarah Catherine Tufts," said Sarah, folding her arms across her chest. "Not girl."

"I'll call you what I like, you little blighter," said Nigel. "And you'll answer straightaway, or get a swift boot in the rear."

Sarah reluctantly unfolded her arms and walked to the door.

"Count yourself lucky, girl," said Nigel, yanking her into the hallway. "I've got another job in need of special talents."

MAYHEM
IN THE MANURE

NIGEL LED Sarah past several closed doors through which she could hear the muffled sounds of children singing and laughing. The winding hallway came to a dead end at a large tapestry of a waterfall. The flowing water looked so lifelike that Sarah thought they would be drenched if they walked any closer.

Nigel swept the tapestry aside and pulled Sarah through. Here the hallway continued as bare walls and a plain stone floor. With the color of Woolie World drained away, everything seemed bleak and full of sharp edges. They turned a few more corners and stopped at an iron door.

"None of them Woolies knows about this door," said Nigel, "and that's how I want to keep it, you hear me?"

"I don't see your worry," said Sarah. "No child would dare go outside after the lies you've told them."

"Master Grim might be right about lopping off your fingers," said Nigel.

Wondering if the fidgety Nigel carried his own pair of scissors, Sarah kept silent as he shoved her out the door.

Outside, the sun had burned away the fog to reveal a raw landscape of stunted shrubs and gnarly trees. The ground rolled up to a distant hill where the salty breeze discouraged all but the most stubborn weeds. Sarah figured the abandoned shantytown lay on the opposite side of the building. Looking to her right, she saw the far horizon with wisps of clouds skimming over a sparkling sea. Looking along the brick wall to her left, Sarah discovered the conveyor belt's final destination, and she scrunched up her nose at the sight of sheep droppings rolling off the belt. Twenty yards away stood a mountain of sheep manure.

"I want you adding them new bits to the old pile," said Nigel. "You got that?"

"This is the job requiring special talents?" asked Sarah.

"Pay attention," said Nigel, handing her a shovel. "If the belt clogs up, the whole operation comes to a standstill. So start shoveling."

"I'll need gloves," announced Sarah.

"What for?"

"I have tender skin," explained Sarah, "and shan't be able to work as hard with blisters."

"Blisters turn into calluses."

"And until then, how shall I hold the shovel?"

"I don't care if you hold it with your ears."

"So Mr. Grim won't mind if my work suffers?" asked Sarah.

"All right, all right, I'll fetch some silly gloves," sniveled Nigel, flapping his hands as he stomped towards the door. "But if you got any ideas about running off, remember, this here's an island. Unless you're a fish, you ain't going nowhere."

Sarah stretched her Woolie suit over her nose and warily approached the conveyor belt. She delicately maneuvered three dried turds onto her shovel and retreated a few steps before risking a shallow breath. Balancing the turds as if they were poisonous frogs about to leap, she advanced on the manure pile and flung the pellets as high as she could. They dribbled down the pile and came to rest.

Sarah leaned on her shovel and admired the wildflowers that flourished around the manure pile. The manure didn't smell that bad once she got used to it, and it wasn't unpleasant at all compared to Mr. Grim's breath or a ship's crew stuffed with beans and cabbage. Or even wet dog fur. Reflecting on the smell of wet fur made Sarah look over her shoulder, but the only thing growling was her stomach.

Shoveling poop didn't take a lot of brainpower, so Sarah reviewed her escape plan. Since she hadn't grown in the last hour, she saw no point in running off to the rowboat that was probably still drifting under the pier. Sarah thought about asking the taller, stronger Thomas to man the other oar, but if the gruff boy wouldn't even talk to her, it appeared unlikely he would help her row to freedom. So her biggest challenge remained convincing Freck that he could step outside without being eaten.

Sarah flung fresh poop onto the manure pile, and it dribbled to a halt. Oddly, several dried nuggets also trickled from a spot several feet away. Sarah stopped to watch as more stale bits rolled from the same area. When a bigger chunk tumbled into the flowers, Sarah dropped her shovel.

"Gophers in gravy boats!"

A tiny hand poked up from the manure pile. The whole arm squeezed through, and then the other arm wormed into sight. The two arms kept digging until a girl's head materialized and her shoulders wriggled into view. Covered in more dirt than a tree root, the button-nosed girl crawled to the surface. She hopped to her feet and sniffed the air. A rope tied around the child's waist dangled to the ground and trailed back into the freshly burrowed hole.

"Good afternoon," said Sarah, guessing the talented digger to be about four years old.

The girl flinched, but didn't say a word. Instead, she shyly looked out the corners of her eyes, as if believing that by simply turning her head she could make herself invisible. Sarah realized that the girl's tattered clothes had once been a Woolie suit.

"Are you some sort of Woolie?" asked Sarah in her friendliest voice.

The girl grabbed the rope around her waist and gave it two quick tugs. The rope's slack disappeared, and the girl hopped back into her hole.

"Wait, please, come back," pleaded Sarah as she raced up the manure pile. "I didn't mean to startle you." Sarah peered down the hole, but the girl was nowhere in sight. "Hello? Are you all right? Everything cheeks high?"

"What are you yelling at?" Nigel had returned with a pair of goldfish orange mittens, and he didn't look pleased to find Sarah separated from her shovel.

"There's a girl down there," said Sarah. "We've got to help her—she'll be squashed to death."

"Quit your fretting," said Nigel. "Them Worms live underground."

"Worms?"

"Nasty things only come up to steal food."

"Children live down there?"

"I'm not real sure where they spend all their time," said

Nigel. "Don't care, neither. Worms is Woolies that couldn't weave, couldn't tend sheep, couldn't even make colors."

"So you just tossed them out?" said Sarah.

"Master Grim don't reward stupidity."

"But that's terrible, that's atrocious, that's, that's . . ." Sarah wasn't sure she knew words severe enough to describe small children being forced to live in the dirt. "That's mortifying—that's inconceivably appalling—"

"That's enough chitchat," said Nigel, throwing the goldfish mittens at Sarah. "Now let's see that shovel move." He stomped back into the building and slammed the door.

Alone again, Sarah looked down the hole. "Hello?"

The tiny bunny girl was long gone.

Thoughtfully, Sarah retrieved the mittens and returned to shoveling poop from the conveyor belt. She was careful not to cover the bunny girl's hole.

BUBBLE SCRUB
AND SWALLOW TIME

A MILLION MILES of conveyor belt poop later, Nigel returned to the manure pile. Sarah couldn't be sure if a smile flitted across his face, or simply another twitch, but she thought he looked pleased with her work. "Time to quit," he barked.

If her arms hadn't been so tired, she would have clapped for joy. Instead, her growling stomach made the only noise as she straggled behind Nigel. He led her inside, down the bare hallway, through the waterfall tapestry, along a maze of corridors, and into a room crowded with chattering Woolies.

The other children were lined up in front of a white porcelain pool overflowing with soapy water. Sarah would have called it a bathtub, but she had never seen any bathtub so enormous. It could easily fit fifty Woolies.

Freck scampered over. "You missed a wonderful-wonderful rug come to life in the weave room," he gushed. "I filled in for a Tweener and had to pull boot-heel black—" Freck stopped to sniff the air. "Have you been riding the conveyor belt?"

"I've been—"

"Working," snapped Nigel. "Now quit running at the mouth and teach her the drill."

"Quick as a Topper, sir," said Freck, taking Sarah's hand and leading her to the bathtub lineup.

"Do we ever eat?" asked Sarah.

"Oh, we gotta bubble scrub before Master Grim lets us have swallow time," said Freck.

"Well, I hope swallow time is soon," said Sarah as she watched fully clothed Woolies step into the water. "Do the children always keep their clothes on when they bathe?"

"Bathe?" said Freck.

"Sorry, bubble scrub," said Sarah. "Do you always bubble scrub while you're still dressed?"

"Master Grim says it's best this way," explained Freck. "This way you bubble scrub you and your Woolie suit the same-same."

Reaching the front of the line, Sarah slipped into the steaming bath and sighed. The heat melted her aches and caressed her wilting body. She gently floated alongside Freck and sighed again at the smell of clean.

"This feels sooooo good."

"A hot bubble scrub is always cozy-snug," said Freck. "Swishing about takes the bamboo from your bones."

As they gradually waded down the bathtub, Sarah spotted the Woolies who had spent the day paddling in the dye vats. Despite bathing, these color bugs were still covered head to toe in green or orange or lavender or some other vibrant color.

"The poor child," Sarah sympathized as she watched a purple boy laugh and splash with the other children. "Imagine how upsetting it must be."

"Why upsetting?" asked Freck.

"Because he looks so . . . so . . . different."

"Color bugs are the same-same as you and me," said Freck.

"Of course they are," said Sarah. "But I'm sure he'd rather be normal."

"What's normal?"

"How things are meant to be," said Sarah. "It's not normal for people to be purple."

"If you make purple string all day," said Freck, "then being purple is full up normal."

"Perhaps," Sarah said with a shrug.

"Feet on the flat," warned Freck as they approached a swarm of Woolies scrubbing bathers with soapy sponges.

Three young girls greeted Sarah, and six whirling arms lathered her every nook and cranny. Sarah giggled and squirmed as sponges tingled her flesh. The girls kneaded wobbly limbs, tickled toes, and befuddled body parts until thick suds covered Sarah and her Woolie suit.

Following Freck's example, Sarah pinched her nose as the three girls gently dunked her beneath the water. More soap bubbles drifted away as Sarah waved good-bye and waded with Freck to the far end of the tub.

Sarah joined Freck in another line where Woolies were being blasted by a hose. The children held out their arms and spun in circles as a jet of water rinsed any remaining soap from their skin and clothes. "Keep your lids down," said Freck, and Sarah squeezed her eyes shut as the water almost knocked her off her feet. Finding her balance, she twirled in the spray until the water streaming from her Woolie suit was clear of suds. Dripping wet, she followed Freck to where Nigel handed out fluffy oversized towels.

Nigel carelessly pitched the towels, and Woolies scrambled to catch them. "Thank you, sir," said Freck, snagging a towel as it sailed over his head.

Nigel tossed a towel in Sarah's direction, but she fumbled it, and the towel dropped into a puddle. A hush fell over the Woolies, and even Nigel stopped his flinging.

"What's the matter?" Sarah asked all the staring faces.

"No one has ever done that," whispered Freck.

"Done what?"

"Dropped it."

"Never?"

"Never ever," said Freck, and nearby Woolies nodded in agreement.

"Well, I'm astonished it doesn't happen all the time," said Sarah. She picked up the soaking towel and politely asked Nigel, "May I have another?"

Nigel looked confused. "Seeing as it's your first time," he said, hesitating, "we'll let it pass."

Shocked Woolies whispered among themselves as Sarah accepted another towel. "Thank you."

"Now, that wasn't normal," whispered Freck as he quickly tugged Sarah by the elbow towards two doors. "I'll meet you on the other side."

In the girls' change room, Sarah hung her laundered Woolie suit to dry, and a pale girl with a sniffly nose helped her find a new suit in her size. When Sarah had finished buttoning the suit's trapdoor, the girl ushered her to more doors and waved good-bye.

In the next large shaggy room, Freck, also in a fresh Woolie suit, handed Sarah a full cup of something white and foamy.

After a long chug she wiped a white mustache from her upper lip. "Mmmmm, I never thought milk could taste so good."

"Milk?"

"It is milk, isn't it?"

"It's glug-glug from the four-leggers," explained Freck.

"Glug-glug. Fair enough," said Sarah. "Whatever you call it, it's delicious. Cheers!" She clanked cups with Freck, and they both finished their sheep's milk.

Freck grabbed bowls and spoons from a long shelf, and they joined a winding lineup of Woolies. At the front of the room, Mr. Grim sat in a lone chair supervising the proceedings.

"Hurry up, hurry up," blustered Mr. Grim. "Spill one drop and you'll be licking it off the floor."

Sarah watched Nigel plunk a bruised apple into a child's bowl and smother it with a ladle of gray gruel. The cold mush hit the bowl with a heavy *thwack*.

"Bullfrogs in butter trays!" gasped Sarah. "What is that?"

"It's swallow time," said Freck.

"But what is it?" said Sarah, not hiding her disgust.

"Same-same as every day," explained Freck. "Apples and glop. What else would you eat?"

Nigel slopped more gruel into another bowl.

"True, one time we got marmalade," Freck admitted, "but Master Grim said it was only 'cuz Nigel's string got tangled and we'd never taste marmalade again, so we'd best forget it." But Freck still smiled at the memory of that sweet orange jam.

"Well, I was hoping for hot roast beef with peas, steaming mashed potatoes, and gravy," sighed Sarah. "Just the way my father likes it."

"Your father?" said Freck.

"Oh yes," said Sarah. "Father says mashed potatoes hold the gravy much better than boiled ones."

"What's a father?" asked Freck.

"Freck, you must know what a father is," insisted Sarah. "A father is a grownup who takes care of you, who keeps you safe. A father is someone who loves you."

"A grownup who's nice?" said Freck. "Sounds like magic."

"Sounds like craziness," grumbled Thomas, who was waiting in the line behind them.

"Oh, but it's true," said Sarah, facing the surly boy.

Thomas scoffed. "Master Grim would be nice enough to tie your ears in a knot."

"I meant in the outside world," said Sarah. "There are plenty of nice grownups in the you-know-where."

"Outside those walls is nothing but wickedness," whispered Thomas loud enough for surrounding Woolies to hear. "I don't know why you think you can tangle Freck's string, but we Woolies know where the knots go."

"Well, Freck, I'm afraid your Thomas isn't quite as clever as you believe," huffed Sarah. "There are still a few knots that he doesn't have straight—"

"Which of you prattling polecats is making all the racket?" asked Mr. Grim, appearing behind the children. Startled Woolies bowed their heads, but Sarah met Mr. Grim's beady eyes.

"It was me," said Sarah as calmly as she could.

"A lot of noise for one person," said Mr. Grim. "I guess your belly ain't interested in a good filling."

"It's not interested in slop."

"Wish I could afford to be so fussy," said Mr. Grim. "I imagine you other Woolies is looking forward to swallow time, ain't you?"

No one said a word.

"Oh come now, I won't bite," said Mr. Grim, strolling among the Woolies. "Thomas, you must fancy a bit of glop?"

"Yes, Master Grim."

"And you, boy?" said Mr. Grim, gently patting Freck's head.

"Been thinking about it all day, Master Grim, sir," said Freck with a quiver in his voice.

"Just as I figured," said Mr. Grim. "Nothing like a tasty fill after a hard day's work. It's a shame your friend's smart mouth is gonna make everyone miss their swallow time."

The Woolies held their empty bowls tighter and looked to

Sarah. She knew Mr. Grim had won, and her shoulders sagged as she mumbled, "Please, sir, I'd like some glop."

"That's better," gloated Mr. Grim. "You still can't have any, but at least your mates won't go hungry."

Sarah muzzled her protest and crossed her arms to hide her clenched fists.

"Now I'll deal with you, boy," said Mr. Grim, turning a bony finger to Thomas. "Where'd you get to this afternoon?"

"Me, sir?"

"Yes, you," said Mr. Grim, poking Thomas's chest. "Is my finger crooked?"

"Master Grim, I was putting new rugs in the done room, sir," said Thomas, backing away from the sharp digit.

"Not when I looked," said Mr. Grim with another stab.

"I also spent time with the puny-news."

"Didn't see you in the nursery, neither."

"And, and," stuttered Thomas, "and I had to check on the four-leggers a time or two."

"You're a hard one to find," said Mr. Grim.

"I'm sorry, Master Grim," said Thomas. "But there's a lot of work to be done."

"And you ain't through yet," said Mr. Grim. "If I got three more puny-new Woolies, and an extra twenty-eight puny-new four-leggers, how many more rugs can you weave?"

Thomas closed his eyes and concentrated. "Eight," he declared. "But not till the puny-news are two heads higher."

"Eight?"

"Yes, sir, eight."

Smack!

Mr. Grim cuffed Thomas in the shoulder. "I don't like waiting for answers," he said. "Now go get your swallow time."

"Yes, sir. Thank you, sir," said Thomas, tugging Freck by the arm and leaving Sarah alone with Mr. Grim.

Luckily, Mr. Grim only snorted once in her general direction and marched back to where Nigel was again serving apples and glop. Sarah shuddered to think what Aunt Margaret would make of a dining room without any tables and chairs. Woolies strolled about as they shoveled gruel into their mouths. All the gulping and slurping surely would have Aunt Margaret asking if these children were raised by wolves. Freck, already done guzzling his dinner, motioned for Sarah to join him as he washed his bowl and spoon in a bucket of soapy water.

"We'd best not give Master Grim any more reasons to droop," whispered Freck, stacking his bowl on a tray to dry.

"I don't believe that dreadful man needs a reason," said Sarah, rubbing her empty tummy.

She followed Freck to more lines of Woolies and shelves stacked with woolen blankets.

"Do I get a pillow?" asked Sarah.

"What's a pillow?" wondered Freck.

"It's big and fluffy," she explained, "and you put your head on it."

"How do you sleep with your head way up in the air?"

"The pillow scrunches down."

"Do I hear more jabbering?" yelled Mr. Grim from the front of the room. "Make me get out of this chair and the lot of you will spend tonight straining the brown barrel."

Sarah wondered why mention of the brown barrel made every Woolie shudder. The threat had Freck scooping two blankets from the shelf and hustling Sarah to a spot on the shaggy floor beside Thomas.

"You'd better learn the rules," said Thomas as they spread out their blankets. "Upset Master Grim and we all suffer. When he's done walloping you, he'll start on the rest of us."

"I'm sorry," said Sarah, crawling under her blanket. "It won't happen again." She hated to apologize to such a despicable boy, but she knew that Thomas was right. Pulling her blanket tighter and staring up at the frosted ceiling, Sarah wondered if anything good would ever happen again. And she wondered how long she could survive without food as her stomach gave another rumble.

"Here," said Thomas, tossing Sarah an apple.

Surprised by the unexpected gift, it took Sarah a moment to respond. Maybe Thomas wasn't so despicable. "Thank you, Thomas. This is extremely kind of—"

"Nobody wants your noisy stomach keeping them awake," said Thomas, not sounding at all kind as he rolled over to sleep.

Sarah crammed the apple into her mouth and concentrated on devouring every morsel from the core.

"I don't care if pillows and mashed potatoes and fathers aren't honest-honest," whispered Freck. "I like your stories."

"But they really are true," said Sarah, also whispering. "Why, if I were home right now, I'd be in a great warm bed with soft pillows and Father would be reading me a bedtime story."

"Fathers sound wonderful-wonderful," said Freck, snuggling closer.

"Father told the best stories," said Sarah as her mind drifted to a faraway place and time. "He would explain why the sun is hot, and why cats sleep in windows, and why pineapples are prickly, and . . . and why he loved me so much."

The memories both comforted and saddened Sarah. "Can't you remember things the way they were, Freck?" she asked. "You know, before you came here?"

"I've always been here," said Freck. "And there are no fathers in Woolie World."

"Then you shall live with me and share mine," said Sarah.

"Honest-honest?" Freck beamed.

"Absolutely honestly," Sarah promised, and Freck's smile grew until his freckles touched.

"Freck, it's time for the long blink," grumbled Thomas from his nearby blanket.

"Cheeks high, Sarah," whispered Freck.

"Corners up, Freck," she replied.

NIGHTTIME VISITOR

BENEATH A moonlit sky, the *Shy Mermaid* wallowed in a dead calm. Canvas sails hung limp, and the ship drifted aimlessly as Lord Tufts stood at the railing peering out to sea. Lost in thought, he barely noticed when Captain Murphy joined him.

"I can't even smell a breeze," said Captain Murphy. "But if we're not moving, neither are them cursed skunks."

He shuffled in place, his boots scraping the deck. "M'Lord, I'll bang on your door the moment they're spotted."

"What makes you think they remain in these waters?" asked Lord Tufts.

"This here's a popular trade route," said Captain Murphy.

"It stands to reason Black Tooth's gonna stay where he can do the most plundering. Yet I admit it's just an old sailor's hunch."

"I trust your instincts, Captain."

"M'Lord, another sailor is assigned the night watch. Why not retire to your cabin?"

"I can't rest knowing those outlaws roam free," said Lord Tufts.

For a long while the two men stood looking out across the vacant sea . . . and Lord Tufts was grateful for Captain Murphy's silent support.

⚓

Meanwhile, back in Woolie World, the dormitory rose and fell with peaceful breathing. Mr. Grim snoozed in his chair, and all the children slept curled beneath their blankets. All the children except Sarah. She lay staring at the high ceiling and its dark glass.

Despite being dead tired, Sarah's jumbled thoughts crowded out any chance of sleep. Images whizzed across her mind as the day's events replayed themselves. One moment she was laughing with her father in Captain Murphy's cabin, the next instant she was bobbing in the ocean beneath a dead pirate, and then she was shoveling poop. Refusing to line up in tidy single file, each memory kept butting to the front of her brain.

She remembered Eagle-Eye Eric coming off his night shift in the crow's-nest and eating his fish stew supper at the same time she ate her boiled egg breakfast. The other sailors claimed Eagle-Eye could spot a dolphin's dimple from a mile away. This impressed Sarah because she often watched the mammals swimming beside the *Shy Mermaid,* and even from up close she couldn't see a dolphin's dimple. Eagle-Eye was the one who had taught her the cleat hitch knot; he told her that sailors take pride in tying the right knot.

Sarah also remembered the *Shy Mermaid* gently rocking her to sleep as she lay in her bunk. That was only one night ago, and now she was sleeping with hundreds of other children.

"Aardvarks and Anglicans!" Sarah blurted out. Six feet away stood Aunt Margaret.

"Well, isn't this disgraceful," clucked Aunt Margaret.

"Shhh," Sarah cautioned. "You'll wake Mr. Grim."

"Good," said Aunt Margaret, tossing her nose even higher towards the ceiling. "I intend to give that ill-mannered brute a piece of my mind. Imagine expecting a second cousin of the king to sleep on the floor!"

Sarah wanted to ask how Aunt Margaret had found her, but it was impossible to squeeze in a word with Aunt Margaret's indignation in full flight. "You were already a handful, and now you're mixed up with these savages." Aunt Margaret rolled her eyes heavenward as if praying for strength to carry on. "From the start I failed to see the wisdom in your being carted off to the colonies."

Sarah knew that Aunt Margaret's "failing to see the wisdom" meant the same as Mr. Grim calling something "daft." Still, Sarah was overjoyed and wanted to give Aunt Margaret a hug—several big hugs—but she couldn't.

Her blanket wouldn't let her.

The more Sarah battled, the tighter her blanket grew until it became a woolen straitjacket. Squirming and kicking, Sarah heard only snippets of Aunt Margaret's lecture. "No better than common animals . . . ill-bred . . . uncultured . . . the outside fork, use the outside fork first . . ."

"I'm sorry for worrying you, Aunt Margaret," cried Sarah, her words spilling out. "And I'm sorry for ever thinking you were mean, because I've met mean people and you're nothing like them. Please, Aunt Margaret, take me home and I promise I'll wear frilly dresses and grow my hair long and forget about hunting bugs and I'll be so proper and refined—"

"Sarah, you're mumbling a lot," whispered Aunt Margaret, but as her face came closer Sarah jerked back—and woke with a gasp. Her aunt had transformed into a freckle-faced boy, and she was tangled up in a blanket on the floor.

"Is everything cheeks high?" Freck asked.

"I'm fine," lied Sarah, jolted back into wakefulness. "Nothing to fret over. My blanket's tangled, that's all."

"Corners up," murmured Freck, and he dropped off to sleep again.

Sarah straightened her blanket and returned to staring at the ceiling. Unable to sleep, she wondered if she was obligated to keep promises made in a dream. She really liked short hair and hunting bugs.

⚓

Early the next morning, the dormitory glowed with the day's first light, but the sun itself remained invisible above the frosted glass. Sarah faintly snored while using Freck as a pillow—

CLANG! CLANG! CLANG!

"ON YOUR FEET, YOU LAZY SNAILS!" Mr. Grim was louder than the ladle and pot lid he clanged together. "GET UP! GET UP! THE LONG BLINK DON'T LAST FOREVER."

"Welcome to tomorrow, Sarah," said Freck.

"Good morning, Freck," yawned Sarah, still hoping that Mr. Grim's bellowing was just another dream. "Though I'm not sure how good it can be with that man's rumpus."

Sarah and Freck folded their blankets and followed the herd of Woolies restacking their bedding on the shelves. Thomas hoisted up Freck so that the smaller boy could put the blankets on a top ledge.

"Comments to yourself today," Thomas warned Sarah in a most unfriendly tone.

"I'm not awake enough to quarrel," said Sarah.

"Then hurry up and get bubble scrubbed," said Thomas, turning on his heels and walking away.

After washing her hands and face, Sarah fetched a bowl and spoon and joined Freck in the breakfast line. Mr. Grim was ladling out another meal of apples and cold glop. Sarah held out her bowl, and the old man plopped an apple in it before hiding the bruised fruit with a slap of mush. Sarah raised the surprisingly weighty meal to her nose and gave a guarded sniff.

"Rather chew on my boot?" growled Mr. Grim.

"Sir, I didn't say a word," said Sarah.

"Good," said Mr. Grim. "Saves me plucking the tongue from your head."

Sarah closed her mouth firmly and walked away to study the glop. The lumps seemed suspicious and the odor unsettling, but since a hungry stomach overrules the eyes and nose, she sampled a spoonful. Her taste buds were stumped. The glop tasted so bland that she could detect no flavor at all. She had several questions for Mr. Grim, but heeding Thomas's advice, she choked back another bite.

"NO LALLYGAGGING OR DILLYDALLYING," Mr. Grim barked at Woolies rinsing their bowls. "A FULL DAY'S

WORK OR THE PIT." The children trembled. "MESS UP AND YOU'LL BE GONE."

"I certainly hope so," Sarah muttered under her breath, but the fright on Freck's face told her that he had overheard. "Don't worry, Freck. You'll be gone, too."

Freck's shock increased even more.

EXPLODING INNARDS

A SHORT TIME later, Sarah ran her hands along the fuzzy wall in the storeroom, searching for the secret door. She found a hinge and traced the door's outline down and around to the other side. Freck scuttled back as she pressed her ear against the door.

"Sounds like blue skies and butterflies," reported Sarah, masking her nerves with an awkward grin. She wriggled her fingers into place and pulled on the door. The door groaned open three inches, and Freck jumped back three feet. Seeing nothing mangy nor menacing outside the gap, Sarah tugged at the door again until she could inch her shoulders through the opening. Cautiously, she stretched her neck to peer left and right.

Sarah laughed for real at the sight of the empty alley. "It's clear sailing!"

But Freck took another step backward.

"Freck, if we have the tiniest problem, we'll jump right back inside," Sarah promised. "I'd never do anything to hurt you. You're my friend."

"My feet are far from the flat," moaned Freck.

"You must at least be curious," said Sarah, extending a hand to him. "It's a wonderful-wonderful world to see. You'll love the real sky and the real sun."

Freck allowed Sarah to gently pull him forward. At the edge of the door, Freck inhaled deeply, closed his eyes, and stepped into the Beyond.

"Well?"

"Everything is so dark."

"You have your eyes shut," Sarah reminded him.

Freck dared to raise one eyelid. Then the other popped open. "There's so much of it—it's everywhere," said Freck. "And it's honest-honest blue!"

Grrrrrrr.

Sarah saw two mangy dogs snarling their way around the corner.

"Easy," she whispered, retreating towards the door. "Don't make any sudden movements."

However, Freck made no movements at all. None. Hypnotized by the dark beasts, he stood rooted to the ground.

"Freck, we really should—"

"MONSTERS!" wailed Freck.

The dogs ripped down the alley as Sarah yanked the screaming boy off his feet and scrambled to the door. Sarah pushed and shoved and heaved, but the door's handle broke off in her hand.

The galloping dogs clawed up a clatter of dirt and stones.

Freck clung to Sarah.

Muscles rippled beneath scruffy fur.

Sarah's fists pounded the door.

Drool flew from gleaming fangs.

"AHHHHHHHHHHHH!"

Sarah rammed the door with her shoulder and toppled inside with Freck on her back. The door clanged shut as the dogs crashed with a *thud* into the other side.

"It's true," sobbed Freck, clutching his thumping heart. "The poison is making my innards explode."

"You're a little excited, that's all," gasped Sarah, panting equally hard. "We'll just have to be more careful next time."

"Oh noooooooo," said Freck, racing for the far door.

"Please, can't we talk about this?" asked Sarah, but the freckled boy was already gone.

Defeated, Sarah wandered among the mountains of yarn and wondered if she would be stuck there forever. She remembered her cousin Julianna who was strong enough to ride any horse in Uncle Alford's stable, and tall enough to place the star atop the Christmas tree, and therefore probably the ideal size to work both oars of the rowboat at once. Julianna had celebrated her eighteenth birthday last autumn. For eleven-year-old Sarah that meant seven more years of cold glop, seven more years of shoveling sheep poop, seven more years of Mr. Grim. Just the thought of it made her tired, and she flopped on a big heap of cabbage green yarn.

"Owwww!"

Sarah sprang to her feet as Nigel crawled out, rubbing his head. "Can't a man have a moment's peace?"

"I'm sorry," said Sarah. "I didn't see you sleeping there."

"I ain't sleeping," said Nigel, rubbing his eyes and stretching a kink from his left leg. "I'm inspecting the string. And just why ain't you out shoveling?"

"I don't feel well," said Sarah, flopping back on the floor.

Nigel blew a quick breath and shooed the air about him. "That's all we need is your foul germs infecting the place."

"I'm not *sick* sick," said Sarah, picking her words. "It's just, well . . . I'm heartsick. I miss my father."

"You know the penalty for gossiping about the Beyond," said Nigel. "I oughta cut off a finger right here and now."

"Perhaps you should," said Sarah, feeling lower than the floor. "I'd rather lose my fingers than forget about Father." A tear trickled down her cheek.

Nigel turned away to scratch his forehead and inspect his elbow. "I'm sure your pa will get on fine without you."

Another tear fell from the corner of Sarah's eye and darkened the cabbage green yarn.

"My pa certainly wouldn't miss me." Nigel shrugged. "Says I'm no more useful than a February pumpkin."

"That's not true—fathers love their children," said Sarah. "If you and your father spent more time together, you'd know that."

"My pa ain't some royal big heart building monuments to me," scoffed Nigel. "My pa's the meanest snake ever slithered about this earth."

Sarah found it hard to disagree. "Still, he must have some redeeming quality," she said, groping for a silver lining. "Surely there's something worthwhile about him."

"What's worthwhile about an old buzzard telling me what to do every minute of every day?"

"Perhaps things were better when you were younger?" suggested Sarah. "Perhaps in the past you did more father-son activities. . . . Not even once?"

"You'd need a sharp noggin to recollect the last time Pa

done some good," said Nigel. But Sarah thought the weaselly man must have been unearthing at least one pleasant memory because his twitches seemed to calm, and he took a seat beside her. "When me and my brother was only knee-high terrors, Pa used to take us on board his ship, the *Golden Barnacle*. Oh, it wasn't so often 'cuz Pa was always too busy, but I remember him teaching me how to read the wind, and how to throw a grappling hook, and how to carry a dagger in my teeth without bloodying up my mouth." Nigel seemed lost in a sweet reflection. "Pa's craftier than you'd think."

"You should talk with him," said Sarah. "Reason with him. What your father's doing isn't right."

"Right and wrong got no place around here."

"I know you care," pleaded Sarah. "Freck said you can be nice. He told me about the marmalade."

"Stupid marmalade mix-up was months ago," Nigel protested as he huffed his way to his feet and returned to twitching and itching. "Give them orange jam one time and they been singing about the fool stuff ever since."

"Please, Nigel, you have to face your father."

"Girl, you gotta face a manure pile," growled Nigel, tugging Sarah to her feet and heading for the door.

Sarah jogged to keep up with her wrist as Nigel jerked her into the hall.

"Ha!" scoffed Nigel, tightening his grip. "No one ever mentions poodle black."

"Poodle black?" asked Sarah as they rushed along.

"Pa's last new color," explained Nigel. "To save us dyeing the yarn black, Pa came up with the brilliant idea of shaving poodle dogs. Best color we ever got from them two dogs is mongrel-muck."

"But those dogs aren't even poodles."

"I warned him," said Nigel, shaking his head. "Never buy black dogs at night."

A group of Woolies scurried from their path. Sarah immediately recognized Thomas because he was the only Woolie who didn't smile and wave. Whipping around another corner, Sarah's nose ran straight into a heavenly odor. She inhaled deeply and trembled at the aroma of fresh baking. Nigel abruptly stopped in front of a door dripping with peach yarn. He didn't appear to be happy with the smells.

"What's wrong?" Sarah asked Nigel as he bit his knuckle.

"What's wrong is inside that room," whispered Nigel. "Look, keep your trap shut and we'll make this quick."

JARRING COLORS

FOLLOWING NIGEL through the door, Sarah glimpsed tall stacks of canned food before closing her eyes to better savor the aromas drifting from a warm stove. Swallowing an excess of saliva, Sarah opened her eyes, and any pleasant thoughts evaporated: Mr. Grim sat hunched over a platter of buttered biscuits and pork sausage, attacking the steaming food with his hands. Grease drizzled down his beard.

"You're late," slobbered the old man around a mouthful of pig. "Swallow time should've been wrapped up long ago."

"Won't be a moment," promised Nigel as he fetched the pot of morning glop from Mr. Grim's cluttered table. The pot sat next to a dirty boot, a filthy sock, and a burlap sack. A tremor of revulsion rippled Sarah's shoulders.

"You should be ashamed," Sarah scolded Mr. Grim. "Innocent children fed a single bowl of gruel, and you sit there feasting."

"Mind your own business," hissed Nigel as he began slopping the leftover glop into the burlap sack.

"It is my business when I'm the one eating gruel."

"What in blazes is she doing here?" asked Mr. Grim.

"I'm dropping the girl off at the conveyor belt."

"Well, don't just laze about out there enjoying the fresh air," said Mr. Grim, smirking at Sarah before cramming more breakfast into his mouth.

"I'm not afraid of hard work," said Sarah. "And I've no desire to end up a Worm."

Mr. Grim spit half a sausage. "You stupid twit!" he yelled, throwing a biscuit past Nigel. "I told you they're all ears."

"She's talking nonsense," cried Nigel as he fumbled the glop ladle.

"It's not nonsense to treat people nicer," said Sarah. "And you could start with your own son. My father would never treat me—"

"I heard after a month you forget you ever had ten fingers," Mr. Grim interrupted.

Sarah balled up her hands behind her back. Mr. Grim returned to chewing with his mouth open, and Nigel's ladle scraped the pot.

Scanning the shelves, Sarah wondered what lurked in the hundreds of dented tins with missing labels. Looking up, she spotted several bags of apples dangling from the rafters. Cages, babies, and now apples.

With a grunt, Mr. Grim pulled his bare foot into his lap and began massaging his toes. "I got another idea for the color room," he said. Sarah gagged as flakes of skin fell like snow.

"What sort of idea?" asked Nigel, tying up the sack of glop.

"Just hear me out," said Mr. Grim, picking at his big toe and carefully peeling off the tip of his yellowed nail. "I was out collecting clamshells for the see-yourself-silver when I stomped on a few frogs—I enjoy that squishy *pop!* sound—and it got me thinking, how about frog-guts green? Brilliant, eh?"

Mr. Grim used the moon-shaped sliver of toenail to free some pork sausage lodged in his back molars.

"Pa, them Woolies got good heads for picking colors."

"The frogs on this island are just going to waste," garbled Mr. Grim. Nearly half his hand was in his mouth, and the noise of scraping enamel gave Sarah goose bumps.

Nigel brushed aside a layer of seaweed and opened an icebox buried in the floor. "But, Pa, what if it turns out like, well, you know."

"You still blaming me for poodle black?"

Nigel seemed to avoid his father's glare as he dumped the sack of glop onto the blocks of ice. "I've got to run her out to the pile."

"Aye," grunted Mr. Grim. "And then you've got to run your arse out there and catch me some frogs."

"But, Pa—"

"But nothing, you lallygagger."

"Slimy frogs," Nigel muttered to himself as he slammed down the icebox lid and pushed Sarah towards the door.

"Stand up to him," whispered Sarah.

"And here, girl." Mr. Grim pitched the disgusting sock at Sarah. "Drop that off in the color room."

"So they can burn it?" asked Sarah.

"Don't be daft," said Mr. Grim. "There's plenty of good life left in that sock."

⚓

Moments later, Sarah trailed Nigel down the hallway. She held the sock pinched in the tips of her fingers and as far as possible from her nose.

"It can't hurt you," said Nigel.

"And neither can your father."

"Enough harping about fathers," said Nigel, grabbing the sock from Sarah and walking a little faster.

"But don't you wish things could be like they were when

you were a boy?" said Sarah, lengthening her strides to catch up. "Like when your father took you sailing?"

"Sailing," laughed Nigel. "Ha!"

"What's so amusing?" asked Sarah.

"Pa wasn't taking me on no pleasure cruise," said Nigel. "He was schooling me on how to be a pirate."

"A pirate?"

"A thieving, murderous, bloodthirsty pirate," explained Nigel as he opened a door. "Not much family fun in that, is there?"

They entered a room crowded with more shelves than a library. Glass jars of liquid color jostled for space on long shelves, and Sarah walked down a row that glimmered with thousands of shades of blue. She read the neatly labeled jars—beneath-your-tongue blue, hold-your-breath blue, melancholy blue, shivering-teeth blue. The containers rattled from the commotion going on beyond the shelves.

"Is it always so noisy?" asked Sarah.

"It's 'cuz them Woolies gotta beat the color outta things," explained Nigel.

At the first color station, Sarah saw Woolies smashing clamshells to smithereens with bamboo hammers. Other Woolies combed their fingers through the oozing clam guts to gather bits of the shells' shiny inside lining—the glossy mother-of-pearl. Other Woolies pulverized these iridescent bits into shimmering silver droplets. Sarah marveled at how the metallic liquid reflected everything around it like a mirror.

"Eight hundred clams get you one jar of see-yourself-silver," said Nigel.

Approaching the next color station, Sarah recognized a pale girl with runny eyes and a red nose. It was the same girl who had helped her in the bubble-scrub change room. Now the weepy girl dumped a bushel of milkweed pods into a press and cranked rollers that squeezed milky juice from the plants.

"That's awful," whispered Sarah.

"You don't like milkweeds?"

"I'm talking about that pitiful girl," said Sarah. "How could you force her to work when she's so sad?"

"She ain't sad."

"She's crying."

"Only 'cuz she's allergic to milkweeds," said Nigel.

"You gave her a job knowing it would make her sick?" said Sarah. "That's despicable."

"Despicable? What's despicable is that the girl's useless when it comes to weaving rugs," said Nigel. "If it weren't for making top-of-the-world white, she'd be tossed out into the dirt."

"To become a Worm?"

"You didn't hear it from me," said Nigel.

Spotting Sarah, the girl waved hello and tried to smile.

"You're doing a wonderful job," said Sarah, peeking into the girl's bucket. The creamy liquid glowed the same shade as the ceiling's frosted glass.

"It's my first ever bucket of top-of-the-world white," said the sniffly girl, blushing.

"Well, it's a perfect match," said Sarah.

"See, runny noses ain't fatal," said Nigel, steering Sarah towards the next color station.

Zing. SPLAT!

A ripe red beet exploded against the wall.

Zing. SPLAT!

Several Woolies launched the vegetables with woolen slings while other Woolies scraped beet bits off the wall and stuffed them into socks. Nigel tossed Mr. Grim's sock to one beet-stained boy who acted as if he had been handed a year's worth of candy. "The socks filter out the chunks," explained Nigel as another Woolie squished his full sock so that a stream of red beet juice filled a jar.

"You need plenty of red," said Nigel. "Red, blue, and yellow are called the 'important' colors 'cuz they can be mixed up to make any other color you want."

Sarah knew they were called primary colors, but she didn't think it a good idea to correct Nigel. Fascinated, she watched Woolies swing their slings in tight circles over their heads and whiz the beets against the wall.

Zing. SPLAT!

Zing. SPLAT!

Zing. SPLAT!

"It looks like fun," said Sarah. "May I try?"

"Slings are more complicated than they look."

"What harm could I do?" asked Sarah. "It appears the whole point is to smash the beets to kingdom come."

"Pick a good ripe one 'cuz they bust up nicer," said Nigel, handing her one of the woolen slings.

Sarah loaded a beet and swung the sling above her head.

"Nothing fancy," said Nigel. "Just aim for the wall."

Zing.

"Oops!"

Sarah's beet shot in the opposite direction.

KAPLUNK!

The stunned milkweed girl wiped cream from her face as she fished the beet from her bucket.

"I'm sorry, I'm sorry," cried Sarah, hustling to the girl. "It's much tougher than I thought."

Sarah grimaced as the bucket of top-of-the-world white turned into pink ripple. "I'm so so sorry."

"I'm sure you'll work the sling wonderful-wonderful after a little practice." The teary-eyed girl smiled. "You shouldn't give up."

"You need a lot more than practice," said Nigel, pushing Sarah across the room. "Now get rid of the bleedin' thing."

Sarah jammed the sling into her pocket as Nigel hurried her across the room past a press that squeezed blueberries into a purple syrup. Sarah popped a berry in her mouth.

"What do you think you're doing?" cried Nigel as he shook Sarah by the shoulders. "Spit it out before it kills you."

"Kills me?"

Sarah saw the other Woolies staring in shock, and she spat out the berry and pulled bits of purple from her tongue. "You mean it's poisonous?"

"But she'll live," Nigel told the Woolies as he hustled Sarah past them. "It was a close one, but she'll be cheeks high. Yes, she'll be corners up, so you can all get back to work."

"I thought it was just a regular berry," said Sarah. "It didn't look any different."

"Keep your mouth still and your legs moving," whispered Nigel as he propelled Sarah towards a far door.

"And it didn't taste any different," continued Sarah.

"If Pa sees you eating them blueberries, he'll—"

"So it was just a harmless blueberry?"

"Poison or no poison," said Nigel, "if Master Grim catches you with purple tonsils, he'll rip them out."

"He's not Master Grim—he's your father."

"Are you listening?" asked Nigel. "Have you understood a word I've said?"

"I understand that a blueberry won't kill you," said Sarah. "And neither will your father. Nigel, you can't be afraid. My father says that honesty is—"

Nigel pounced on Sarah and dragged her by the scruff of the neck. "I told you, my pa ain't nothing like yours," he hissed, heading towards a large barrel separated from everything else. "My pa is just like the brown barrel." Nigel lifted the lid and held Sarah's face within inches of the rancid sheep organs inside. A single whiff made her cheeks bulge. Her morning glop was in danger of reappearing. "Just like the brown barrel, my pa is rotten to the core."

"Please, please," Sarah begged as the stench invaded her nostrils.

"Squeeze my pa and you'd get ten barrels of brown."

"I'm sorry," gasped Sarah. "Please, I'm sorry."

Nigel shoved her away and slammed down the brown barrel's lid. "You'll be sorrier if we gotta have this chat again."

DIVING HEADFIRST

NOTICING THAT his facial twitches were excessive, even for Nigel, Sarah only risked a silent nod when Nigel ordered her to the manure pile. "Two rights and a left and you'll find the waterfalls," he seethed before storming off in the other direction.

Sarah turned the first right and bumped into a Woolie.

"Freck!" she gushed. "How are you?"

"The puny-news need covering," mumbled Freck, keeping his head down as he showed Sarah three pairs of light green booties.

"They're beautiful," said Sarah, changing direction to walk alongside the boy.

"Bug-belly green is a good color for puny-news," Freck sheepishly agreed. "Better than big-tree green or bad-teeth green or murky-pond green or—"

"Is it ever just plain green?"

"What does plain look like?"

"I'm not really sure," said Sarah as they took another turn. "Freck, I'm awfully sorry about this morning."

The boy only lowered his head more.

"I truly believed it was safe," explained Sarah.

"Them six-leggers would swallow me in two bites," said Freck.

"Actually, they have four legs."

"Honest-honest?" said Freck. "I didn't think anything could run that fast with only four legs."

"We moved pretty fast."

"And I cried like a puny-new," confessed Freck, and his head dropped farther south.

"I don't blame you," said Sarah. "It was scary."

"You're better off without me," said Freck. "I can't help untangle your knots 'cuz I'm not . . ."

"You're not what?"

"I'm not brave," said Freck, and his chin sank onto his chest.

"Nonsense," said Sarah. "Not wanting to be ravaged by wild beasts doesn't make you a coward. It makes you absolutely normal."

Freck didn't seem convinced, but his head didn't look as heavy.

"I'm sure you're terribly brave," said Sarah. "After all, you had the courage to step outside and breathe blue air."

"It wasn't really blue," said Freck as his chin floated higher.

"You didn't know that then," said Sarah. "And yet you faced unknown danger. In fact, I wouldn't be surprised if you grow up to be as brave as my father."

"You think so?" said Freck, stopping at the nursery's door.

"Most definitely," declared Sarah, happy that her friend's head rested back atop his shoulders.

Freck opened the nursery door.

"Jackals and Jacobites!" whispered Sarah, jumping for cover. "He's in there."

"He's the one who ordered the coverings," whispered Freck.

Sarah peeked inside. Like a doting grandfather, Mr. Grim fussed over the three happy babies gurgling in their cocoons, entertaining them with tickles and tongue clicking. "Has my sweet angel got cold tootsies?" he cooed while lightly tweaking a baby's toes. Hands so used to poking, pinching, and punching had become tender.

"Cheeks high till swallow time," whispered Freck as he waved good-bye and stepped through the door. Sarah heard the boy clear his throat to announce his presence, and she watched the old man stiffen and scowl.

Now, that's bravery, Sarah thought as she closed the door.

Winding through the maze of hallways, Sarah wondered how she would find her way back to the kitchen's peach-colored door. The hallways appeared to be color-coded, but she didn't know the code. Aware that Mr. Grim was occupied back in the nursery, Sarah felt it safe to peek behind one of the many other peach doors.

Sarah found a class of bright-eyed three-year-olds rolling on the floor, attempting to tie knots while somersaulting through a tangle of yarn.

"Blue rugs need slower songs," said their teacher, who looked about eight years old. "You can't rush a blue rug." The girl waved hello to Sarah and continued her lesson. "Yellow rugs need sunny, happy songs. And who can tell me about red rugs?"

Every student raised an arm, and the teacher pointed out a pint-sized boy.

"Red rugs are hot and passionate," answered the boy as if reciting from memory. "They need fast songs to raise the heat."

"Corners full up," said the teacher, and other little heads nodded in agreement.

"How come we don't learn any black songs?" asked another eager student.

"Black is such a corners-down color," explained the teacher. "Last time we wove an entire rug out of hole-bottom black, no one showed their chewers for a week. So unless Master Grim asks special, we don't bother with gloomy colors. Now, let's practice our song for morning-pee yellow."

The Woolies burst out singing and, despite the color's name, the song for weaving morning-pee yellow was happy and sunny. Sarah liked it so much that she listened to nine verses before she waved good-bye and backed out the door.

After two more turns, Sarah's nose detected a hint of sausage, and she knew she was finally headed in the right direction. She made sure she was alone and slunk through the peach-colored door.

Inside the pantry, Sarah quickly lowered a sack of apples from the rafters and chose the best ones to stuff into her pockets.

⚓

Outside on the mountain of manure, Sarah placed an apple where the bunny girl had tunneled to the surface. Placing other apples farther and farther away, Sarah laid a trail of five apples leading to flat land.

Satisfied with her plan, Sarah crouched behind a nearby shrub and waited . . . but since watching a manure pile becomes awfully boring awfully fast, Sarah decided to kill time by practicing with her woolen sling. A clump of dirt made a perfect substitute for a ripe red beet.

Swinging the sling in tight circles over her head, she aimed at a wildflower.

Zing.

Her clump missed the flower by twenty feet. So, reloading her sling and swinging it over her head again, Sarah searched for a bigger target. This time she aimed at a shrub.

Zing.

She missed by forty feet. Reloading her sling, Sarah searched for an even bigger target and aimed at a tree.

Zing.

"Ouch!"

The clump of dirt smacked her foot.

Deciding she should kill time without killing herself, Sarah pocketed the sling and resumed spying on the manure pile. She waited and waited. A droning buzz orbited her head, and Sarah swatted at a fly. As time passed, she began to doubt her plan. After someone discovered the unpleasantness of crawling through manure, wasn't it ridiculous to expect her to do it a second time? Perhaps Aunt Margaret had been wrong when she said, "Most people commit the same mistakes over and over again." But it was one of the rare times when Sarah's father had agreed with his sister.

"Chinchillas and chinaware!" whispered Sarah as loose bits trickled from the hole in the manure pile.

Slowly, the top of a head emerged, and then two eyebrows wriggling over two darting brown eyes. The same frail bunny girl from the day before twitched her button nose. Sarah squeezed behind the shrub as the child crawled to the surface and hopped into a crouch. The girl's head snapped east and west. Again, a rope tied around her waist trailed back into the hole.

The bunny girl scooted three quick steps and stopped. Her neck stretched as she inhaled the breeze and straightened her legs. Blinking away the sun, the girl spied the first polished red apple. Sarah anxiously clutched fistfuls of leaves as the girl drew back half a step. The girl pulled more slack rope from the hole, and Sarah released her stranglehold on the shrub.

With greater freedom to move, the girl hopped to the first apple. Her head jerked to the next apple and then the next apple as she picked out the trail of fruit. Sarah watched the odd creature hesitate and survey the manure pile before scooping up the first piece of fruit.

Sarah's legs ached from folding herself into such a small ball, but she stayed behind the shrub as the girl collected more apples. By the fourth apple, the girl had ventured so far from the manure pile that Sarah could only see her back. Upon retrieval of the fifth apple, Sarah sprang from her hiding spot and zipped between the girl and her escape hole.

"I tried to pick the best ones," said Sarah.

The bunny girl froze, and the apples tumbled to the ground.

"Please, you must take them," said Sarah.

The girl remained silent as a fence post.

"They're a gift," said Sarah, bending down to pick up the two closest apples. "I tried to find some marmalade, but I'm afraid these are the best I could do."

Sarah took a few slow steps and gently set the apples one at a time into the girl's unmoving arms. The girl's wide eyes followed Sarah's every movement. From this close Sarah could see her pale lips tremble beneath the dirt.

"I mean no harm," Sarah assured her as she loaded the girl with three more apples. "Truth be told, I'm hoping there's a way we can help each other."

Still, the girl only stared, and Sarah considered another possibility. "Do you and I speak different languages?"

But Sarah never found out the answer, for the girl bolted amid a fountain of apples that splashed off Sarah's feet.

"Wait! Please!" cried Sarah as the girl scrambled up the manure pile clutching one last apple. "I just want to talk."

The girl jumped down her hole and Sarah lunged for the spooled-out rope, but with a flick it disappeared, too.

FISHING WITH WORMS

IMMEDIATELY, SARAH took a quick breath and jumped into the hole. After a short drop, she hit solid ground and found herself in a tunnel, where musty air chilled her lungs. The yellow glow of an oil lamp revealed timbers that propped up the ceiling of the underground passage. Other lamps were too far apart to illuminate the entire length of the tunnel, and Sarah only caught glimpses of the bunny girl as she followed her through dwindling light. Thick dust blackened Sarah's feet, and she recalled Mr. Grim telling Captain Murphy about the abandoned coal mines.

Tunnels branched off everywhere the miners had chased their coal, and the little girl kept zigzagging in new directions. Someone somewhere must have been reeling in the rope tied around her waist because any slack rope disappeared as soon as it fell. Stumbling to keep up, Sarah raced through a dark patch.

"Please, stop," she cried, her voice slapping off bare rock walls. "I just want to talk."

The bunny girl's silhouette hurried around another corner.

"At least slow down," panted Sarah, groping her way through the bend. She shivered at the feel of pitiless cold stone.

Up ahead, the girl turned at a lamp and vanished into the rock. But when Sarah reached the spot, she realized the dusty ray of light did not shimmer from a miner's lantern, but from a small gap in the tunnel wall. Crouching low, Sarah stepped through the opening.

"Rabbits and royalty!"

Sarah stood in a cave filled with the dozens of Woolies that Mr. Grim had tossed away. Like the bunny girl, these Worms stepped back without ever taking an eye off Sarah. Mouths hung open without ever making a peep. The only sound came from a breeze gusting through a hole in the far wall—a natural window in the rock that allowed a spectacular view of the ocean ninety feet below.

Recalling one of Aunt Margaret's many lectures on social graces and first impressions, Sarah pulled back her shoulders and stood tall. "Hello, everyone," she said with a smile. "I'm Sarah."

Sarah noticed that the bug-eyed little boy who had been collecting the bunny girl's rope continued to inch backward.

"Don't be afraid," said Sarah. "I'm quite harmless. . . . Really."

No one seemed to believe her.

"Can't you mind your own business?" The question came from deep in a corner.

"But we're facing the same dilemma," explained Sarah, walking towards the voice. "Doesn't that put us together in the same business?"

More Worms scurried from her path.

"Chameleons and cameos!"

Thomas was kneeling in front of a small boy, cleaning the child's scraped shin.

"Thomas?" sputtered Sarah. "Thomas, why are you here?"

"You'll mend up healthy as a sea horse," Thomas assured the Worm without a single glance in Sarah's direction.

Sarah felt as invisible as the last time she had sat in Aunt Margaret's front parlor. Still, she thought, the people on this island might benefit from one of her aunt's etiquette lectures. "Thomas, what are you doing in the Beyond?" Sarah asked while promising herself she would be better behaved the next time she had tea with Aunt Margaret . . . if she ever saw her aunt again.

"Try to keep the dirt off it," Thomas gently instructed as he carefully wrapped the child's leg and continued to ignore Sarah.

"What about all your nothing-but-wickedness speeches?"

Thomas still didn't look at her.

"We'll check it again tomorrow," said Thomas as he got to his feet.

"Thank you, Thomas," said the Worm.

"Cheeks up, now," said Thomas, playfully tousling the Worm's hair. But turning to Sarah the tenderness drained from his voice. "What if Master Grim comes looking for you?" he snarled. "You're not only a fool, you're dangerous."

"Thomas, I don't understand," said Sarah. "Why don't you tell the others about the Beyond? Why don't you tell them the truth?"

"You want me to tell Freck he can come live in the dirt?" asked Thomas. "Or should I tell him useless rubbish about fathers he won't ever see?"

"But I'm taking Freck with me," Sarah explained. "I know where I can get my hands on a rowboat and we'll—"

"That's your brilliant plan?" said Thomas. "Cross the ocean in a rowboat? A six-foot boat against sixty-foot waves? Your self-ishness will get you both killed."

"Selfishness?"

"If you weren't always thinking of yourself, you might see what's best for Freck," said Thomas. "Now get back to Woolie World before Master Grim figures out you're missing."

Sarah stammered and her face turned red, but she couldn't think of a good response. Perhaps crossing the ocean in a rowboat was a bit risky, but what else could she do?

"Move it," said Thomas.

"I'm not going back to that evil man," said Sarah.

"You've no say in the matter."

"I'd rather be a Worm than a slave."

"You wouldn't fit in."

"Sure I would," insisted Sarah.

"Out here we have to work together," said Thomas. "We depend on each other. Don't we, Dee Dee?"

Dee Dee, the bunny girl, appeared uncomfortable at being suddenly included in the debate. Her timid shrug seemed more of an apology to Sarah.

"I'd do my part," promised Sarah.

"Forget it," said Thomas, heading towards one of the many tunnels that exited the cliff-side cavern.

Sarah wished she had enough muscles to knock Thomas on his smug behind, but she settled for grabbing Dee Dee's rope and wrapping it around her own waist. The other Worms started to murmur, and Thomas turned back.

"What do you think you're doing?"

"Proving I can fit in," said Sarah, securing the rope around her middle with an Eagle-Eye cleat hitch knot that she hoped would dazzle Thomas.

Thomas didn't notice Sarah's excellent knot. Worse, he laughed at her. "You fancy it's that easy?"

"I'm willing to work," said Sarah. "And I'm as able to crawl through tunnels as anyone else here."

"Well, that's great, then," said Thomas. "Maybe you'd like to fetch the Worms their swallow time. I bet they'd really enjoy a no-legger."

Dee Dee's eyes flashed with concern.

"Corners up, corners up," said Thomas, calming the child. "Sarah has her heart set on being a Worm."

"You expect me to catch a shark?" asked Sarah.

"Just a wee no-legger," said Thomas. "You call them fish."

"Isn't it a little dry up here for fish?"

"You'll find them at the end of number four," said Thomas, pointing to another narrow exit.

"Really?" said Sarah, looking to Dee Dee for confirmation.

Dee Dee nodded a reluctant yes.

"As soon as you've got one," said Thomas, "give a tug and we'll reel you in."

As Sarah headed towards the dim tunnel, the Worms

scurried to anchor the rope from her waist to a large boulder. She didn't think it was a good sign that the Worms looked so serious. Sarah's heart thumped against her rib cage, but she wasn't going to let Thomas see her fear. "What kind of stupid fish lives in the dirt?" she grumbled, figuring that grumbling always made Mr. Grim seem tougher.

Within moments, Sarah had stepped beyond the sunshine of the cave, and she paused until her eyes adjusted to the darkness. Squinting only helped so much, and soon she fumbled her way by touch. With the cold rock against her hand, Sarah felt the cramped tunnel slope downwards at an ever sharper angle. She was thankful for each twitch of the rope around her waist because it meant that the Worms were still holding on to the other end.

Sarah lost her footing as the tunnel became an almost vertical drop, and she rattled like a pebble sliding through twists and turns.

"Whoooooooooa!"

A burst of sunlight appeared, and Sarah shot into space.

TUG OF WAR

SARAH PLUNGED so fast towards the ocean that rushing wind stuffed the scream back into her throat and the water became a blue blur racing up to meet her.

"ULP!"

Her rope snapped tight, and Sarah sprang back like a dog unexpectedly reaching the end of its leash. Yo-yoing ten feet above the surf, she blinked the ocean's mist from her eyes and tried to slow her heart. With the taste of salt water again in her mouth, her relief hardened into resentment. She tugged on the rope, and slowly she was reeled in—moving upwards in three-foot jerks until she had grappled her way back into the cliff's tunnel.

Retracing her way through the darkness, Sarah traveled only as fast as the unseen Worms could haul in her rope. Fine, she thought, it gives me time to practice my speech for Thomas. She certainly would give that infuriating young scoundrel a piece of her mind. Then again, perhaps mere words—however scathing—would be wasted on such a calloused scourge of a boy. Perhaps a better strategy would be simply to march past Thomas without uttering a single syllable. Sarah was still debating the proper approach when Dee Dee met her at the edge of the light.

"Sorry," whispered the bashful girl as she helped untie the rope around Sarah's waist.

"It wasn't your doing," said Sarah, taking Dee Dee's hand and marching back into the Worms' cave.

"Empty-handed?" asked Thomas as if nothing unusual had happened.

"You're no better than Mr. Grim," fumed Sarah. "I could have been killed."

"Get moving," said Thomas. "We've already been gone too long."

The second last thing in the world Sarah wanted to do was return to Mr. Grim, but the last thing she wanted to do was beg Thomas to stay. Sarah felt a tug on her arm and turned to see Dee Dee offering her the apple.

"Thank you, Dee Dee," said Sarah gently. It wasn't the girl's fault if Thomas was a reptile. "But that apple is meant for you."

"I'll go back for the others," whispered Dee Dee, pressing the red fruit into Sarah's hand.

"Hurry up," barked Thomas.

"It was very nice to meet you, Dee Dee," said Sarah, pocketing the apple. "I'll save it for a snack."

⚓

Thomas spoke over his shoulder as Sarah trailed him through the tunnels. ". . . Because I doubt he'd have checked past the pile—not with him being so lazy."

Still pouting, Sarah refused to acknowledge Thomas.

"Did you hear me?" he said. "If Nigel did come looking for you, you've got to tell him you were having a pee behind the trees."

"I'll tell the man what I please," said Sarah.

"Do you want his boot or mine?"

Sarah only huffed.

"Don't think I'd do it?" asked Thomas.

"My aunt would be greatly disappointed if I said what I think you're capable of."

"Why are you such a spoiled brat?" asked Thomas.

"Why are you such a pigheaded bully?" asked Sarah, quickly forgetting about Aunt Margaret's great disappointment.

"Just get your backside to the weave room."

"There's more to life than making rugs for Mr. Grim."

"Not for you," said Thomas. "Not anymore, and the sooner you accept it, the less grief there'll be for all of us."

"What I do is no concern of yours," argued Sarah. "I'll make sure you don't miss your precious glop."

"I can handle an empty stomach or the odd beating," said Thomas. "What I won't stand for is you tangling Freck's string and cramming his head full of crooked-feet schemes."

"He should know the truth."

"The truth is you can't cross the ocean in a rowboat."

"The truth is there's a better world out there," said Sarah, "and Freck should hear about it."

"Why?" said Thomas as he whirled around to block Sarah's path. "So Freck can hope for things he'll never get? Hope for places he'll never go? Hope for family he'll never see? Hope and hope and hope until it breaks his heart."

"I would never hurt Freck," said Sarah.

"Your stupid hope will do that for you," said Thomas, and he marched away leaving Sarah feeling as if she'd been punched in the stomach. With nothing more to say, they carried on through the winding tunnels in silence until Thomas stopped and sniffed the air. "Something smells funny," he said.

"This whole island smells funny," said Sarah.

"Shhh," said Thomas. The odor grew stronger as they moved towards a darker section of the tunnel.

"It smells like oil," said Sarah.

"For once I think you're right."

Sarah ignored Thomas's sarcasm because she was remembering something she once overheard in the ship's galley. "One fire and we'll be sucking mud off the bottom of the sea," Captain Murphy had warned the cook lighting the stove. "It'd almost be safer to starve than carry that cursed oil." Whether on a ship or in the bowels of an island, Sarah knew that an oil fire was equally perilous.

Thomas proceeded with cautious tightrope-walker steps while Sarah's nerves made her chattier. "I wonder how many of these tunnels there are—I'm sure a person would have difficulties counting that high—the island is a bit like Swiss cheese." And she forced a nervous chuckle. "You see, Swiss cheese has—"

Thomas's foot landed with a small *splash*.

"Please tell me that's water," said Sarah.

"I wish I could," said Thomas, rubbing his fingertips in a trickling stream of liquid.

"Perhaps one of the lanterns has a leak," suggested Sarah.

"SHOW YOUR FACES!"

Mr. Grim's voice boomed through the tunnels.

"Coyotes and crumpets!" whispered Sarah.

"WIGGLE UP HERE NOW, OR YOU WORMS IS GONNA GET MIGHTY HOT."

Thomas grabbed Sarah's hand and raced back through the darkness.

ROASTING ALIVE

Aboveground in a bumpy field, Nigel emptied a barrel of oil into a tunnel entrance. He had little stomach for the job, but his father held a torch and eagerly waited like a child on Christmas Eve.

"See how it's blue at the bottom?" said Mr. Grim, admiring the torch's dancing flame. "It's 'cuz it's the hottest part."

"I imagine the whole thing's far from cozy-snug."

"You know, it takes longer than you'd think for a man to burn to death," explained Mr. Grim. "It's 'cuz he dies from the outside in."

"I ain't thought about it much," said Nigel.

"Have you ever eaten human flesh?" wondered Mr. Grim. "Don't roll your eyes at me, boy. I was very hungry at the time."

Nigel worked up his courage as he shuffled behind his father. He tried to sound as if the idea had just arrived at that moment. "Pa, you ever thought about taking a little time off?"

"To do what?" asked Mr. Grim.

"I don't know," said Nigel, and he hemmed and hawed for a bit. "Maybe we could take a trip—go fishing."

"And leave them little blighters on their own so they can destroy everything I've worked for?"

"I was just thinking—"

"You wasn't thinking too hard." His father cupped his hands around his mouth and roared into the tunnel. "SHOW YOUR FACES, YOU SCHEMING LITTLE DEVILS!"

Nigel twitched and shooed a fly from his mustache.

"She's beautiful," sighed Mr. Grim.

"The new girl?"

"No, you daft fool," said Mr. Grim. "That fly buzzing about your lip."

"A fly?"

"Look at its hind end," said Mr. Grim. "Look at that beautiful blue glow. It'd make a great rug color."

"Fly blue?"

"Shiny-hiny blue," said Mr. Grim. "Sounds more poetic."

"Pa, I think the Woolies do pretty well on their own."

"They're my bloody rugs, and I can't even suggest a bloody

color?" Mr. Grim's failure at color selection was a sore point, and again he roared into the tunnel. "YOU SEA LICE GOT TEN SECONDS!"

Nigel shuffled some more while Mr. Grim squinted into the dark hole. "But, Pa, why don't we ever do things together?"

"We're together right now."

"I mean father-son type things."

"What type of shenanigans?"

"You know, family stuff," said Nigel, laboring to explain. Discussing emotions was totally new to him. "I just figured you and me could be, I don't know, closer."

"Closer?"

"As a family."

"We're blowing up this tunnel together," said Mr. Grim. "Ain't that a family outing?" And he tossed the torch in the hole.

WHOOOOSH!

The oil exploded in a giant fireball, and Nigel scuttled back from the blast of heat. His pa danced a jig in the middle of a huge belch of black smoke.

⚓

Underground in the Worms' cave, above the children's confused panic, Sarah heard the *pop* of glass. She imagined the miners' lamps shattering in the intense heat as the raging fire devoured the stream of oil. She watched Thomas standing on the shoulders of two smaller boys as he tied a rope around the support beam over one of the cave entrances.

"You're sure it's this one?" asked Sarah.

"It'd better be," said Thomas, yanking the rope tight and jumping to the ground. "Everyone on my count," he ordered as Sarah and the rest of the Worms grabbed the rope. "One, two three—pull!"

The children strained to wrench the support beam from the roof, but the large timber wouldn't budge. The air grew hotter, and Sarah spit the taste of burning oil from her tongue.

"Harder," urged Thomas.

Sarah dug in her feet and gritted her teeth. The exploding oil lamps sounded closer, but the support beam wasn't moving.

"Harder," groaned Thomas, and Sarah pulled the rope with every scrawny muscle she had. Sweat drenched her body, tears stung her eyes, and the rope blistered her hands. Sarah could feel the Worms pulling around her and knew that survival depended on winning this tug of war.

Dust and dirt drifted from the ceiling as the support beam slowly shifted.

"HARDER!" pleaded Thomas.

Sarah heard a hissing noise and looked up to see a wall of fire screaming towards the cave. The greedy inferno sucked every speck of oxygen from the air. Dry timbers sizzled and exploded into flames.

The Worms gave a desperate heave. The support beam snapped, and the children tumbled back in a heap as a great rumble of rock fell from the ceiling. Plumes of dirt and dust blotted out the light. Sarah held her breath and blindly faced the creaking wall. A tiny hand slipped inside her own, but no one else stirred. Gradually, a fresh breeze from the cliff opening chased away the dark to reveal a solid pile of stone quietly sealing the entrance. Dee Dee smiled at Sarah and squeezed her hand. Together they exhaled, and the cave erupted as cheering Worms helped each other to their feet and began dancing. Ignoring her stinging palms and aching muscles, Sarah shared hugs with other children. In the middle of a twirl, Sarah noticed a somber Thomas heading towards another of the cave's exits.

"Where are you going?" she asked.

"This isn't your concern," said Thomas, but Sarah knew that this time he wasn't being mean or petty.

"Thomas, you can't go up there," said Sarah.

"It's only a matter of time till Master Grim has another go at it," said Thomas.

"Then we'll seal that exit," reasoned Sarah.

"And the next and the next?" said Thomas. "We'd only end up trapped in here."

"Don't be crazy," said Sarah. "If you show your face above-ground, he'll kill you."

"And if I stay down here, he'll kill us all."

"Thomas," whispered Dee Dee, "please don't go."

And then every Worm spoke at once, urging Thomas to stay.

"Hush," said Thomas. "No time for drooping. Feet on the flat." But as he turned to leave, the Worms mobbed the much taller boy and hugged Thomas from all sides. Some reached his waist, and smaller Worms just wrapped their arms around a leg.

"Take care of each other," said Thomas, his voice breaking.

Surrounded by sniffles and wet faces, Sarah felt her own heart flood with helplessness. "What have I done?" she fretted as Thomas gave Dee Dee a final squeeze good-bye and disappeared into a tunnel. "What have I done?" She couldn't stand in one place, and the ocean's cool breeze now chilled her. She struggled to fill her lungs. "What have I done?"

⚓

Thomas crawled to the surface and lay in the tall weeds while his eyes adjusted to the sunlight. The ground felt cool and refreshing through his Woolie suit, and he welcomed the rich smell of grass after the stink of burning oil.

"FOOL, YOU CAN'T SEE NOTHING FROM THERE!"

Thomas cringed at the closeness of Mr. Grim's rant.

Propping himself up on his elbows, Thomas spotted Mr. Grim, Nigel, and a blackened tunnel entrance forty yards to his left. Nigel scratched his head as he knelt peering into the tunnel.

"GET YOUR MELON RIGHT IN THERE," roared Mr. Grim, kicking the burnt earth at Nigel's backside.

Thomas couldn't work out Nigel's mutterings as he flapped his arms and poked his head farther into the hole.

Knowing he could delay matters no longer, Thomas popped to his feet. "I wish you were dead!" he screamed, hoping he sounded hysterical enough. "You're cruel, wicked beasts."

"FETCH ME THAT BACKSTABBER!" commanded Mr. Grim, and Nigel scrambled towards Thomas.

Thomas sped through the field, but looking over his shoulder, he slowed when the gap between him and his pursuers grew larger. Thomas had expected the skinny Nigel to be faster. It was no surprise that Mr. Grim trailed behind cursing.

Running over a flat stretch, Thomas searched for soft ground and crumpled onto a patch of grass. Rolling back and forth clutching his ankle, he faked a few sobs.

"You're just as evil," he cried as Nigel skidded to a stop beside him. The twitching Nigel hovered over Thomas and waited for a breathless Mr. Grim to arrive.

"Who else is down there?" said Mr. Grim, kicking Thomas in the ankle.

"They're dead," spat Thomas. "You killed them all, you worthless coward."

"I don't believe you," snarled Mr. Grim. "Hold him down."

Thomas squirmed, but Nigel sat on his chest and pinned his shoulders.

"Keep him still," barked Mr. Grim, ripping a clump of grass from the ground.

Nigel gripped Thomas's ears, and though he strained red with effort, Thomas couldn't move an inch. From the corner of his eye, Thomas watched Mr. Grim select a single blade of grass.

"I always knew you was trouble," hissed Mr. Grim, getting on his hands and knees beside Thomas. "Thinking you're too clever for the rest of us."

"I swear no one else is down there," sobbed Thomas. "It's the truth."

"I'll find me the truth," said Mr. Grim. "Scratch your brain and I'll get all the truth I want."

Thomas scrunched his face, but couldn't stop the blade of grass that Mr. Grim shoved up his nostril. The innocent tickle turned into excruciating torture. His eyes boiled into watery pools as the grass drilled into his head. Thomas screamed and snorted, and Nigel held tight.

"Who else is down them tunnels?" Mr. Grim croaked in his face.

"No one," cried Thomas, now with real tears.

"Where's the girl?"

"You killed her," blubbered Thomas. "You killed them all."

"Boohoo and I'll miss you, too. Hey!"

Nigel released his grip, and Thomas wriggled out from under him, gasping for air and rubbing his nose. Not even thinking about running, Thomas hid his face in the dirt and wept.

"Why'd you let him go?" snarled Mr. Grim.

"The girl's gone and you know it," said Nigel.

"Yeah, but wasn't you having fun?" said Mr. Grim, his lips curling into a thin smile. "Wasn't it a real father-son type experience?"

⚓

Freck happily sang along as Woolies created another rug in the weave room. The kneeler-deep mishmash of mostly red yarns included crab apple red, cardinal red, and autumn red. As Woolies cartwheeled and crawled past, Freck wondered if crab apples, cardinals, and autumns might be the names of other things like Sarah's sky blue. Still, that didn't stop him from singing his heart out. After all, he knew that red rugs are hot and passionate and need fast songs to raise the heat.

Waddling lower than the Toppers and above the Undies, Freck pulled a strand of tongue red, a slightly purplish color with a thin coating of white only visible in the morning. Following the song's advice, Freck hopped and hopped and twirled before trading his yarn for another Woolie's strand of cut-lip red. Overhead, Toppers zipped past with strands of mud-puddle, which Freck knew is darker than behind-the-ear or dirty-kneeler brown. Freck wondered if the streaks of brown would end up becoming a twig in the final design.

The doors burst open, and Freck dropped his strand.

Mr. Grim dragged Thomas inside by the ear. Thomas kept his eyes on the floor as he whimpered in pain. Nigel followed behind huffing and shaking his head.

"Ready the pit!" barked Mr. Grim. Panic swept over the Woolies as everyone stared in disbelief. Going nose to nose with a small motionless boy, Mr. Grim screamed, "NOW!"

Unfortunately, that small boy peed in his Woolie suit, but Freck and the other Woolies sprang to action—rolling up the lumpy not-yet-a-rug yarn and pulling back the shaggy carpet. Helping to remove a heavy plank, Freck tried not to look down at the pit's pool of rippling black. He shivered when he heard the cranking of the winch and the bamboo cage slowly dropping from the rafters.

Mr. Grim threw Thomas into the cage and wedged the iron pin into the lock. Thomas desperately fought the bamboo bars, and the loud rattling flooded Freck with horrible memories.

Surrounded by terrified Woolies, Freck conquered his fear enough to speak. "But, Master Grim, what did Thomas do?"

"Don't ask questions," growled Mr. Grim. "Apples—I caught him thieving apples. Now quit your yammering."

Normally, Freck wouldn't dream of contradicting Mr. Grim, but with Thomas hovering above hungry no-leggers, talking back didn't seem so heroic. "Master Grim, sir, you must be wrong," said Freck. "Thomas would never be a frown-maker. Thomas is the least frown-maker in all of Woolie World."

"Oh, that's what he'd like you to believe," said Mr. Grim. "But he would steal the breath from your lungs if he had the chance. Thomas couldn't care less if you other Woolies lived or died."

Freck refused to believe it. He knew Mr. Grim's string was in a terrible muddle, but he had no time to convince him.

"LOWER THE CAGE!" commanded Mr. Grim.

Two sad Woolies slowly cranked the winch, and the cage jerked downwards. Sinking into the pit, Thomas stopped fighting the bamboo bars and turned pale. Freck's chest ached at the sound of hungry no-leggers swimming in circles; the scaly beasts were ready for swallow time.

GRAND OPENING

"MR. GRIM'S a liar!" cried Sarah, standing defiantly on the far side of the weave room. A confused buzz traveled through the Woolies, and the two children cranking the winch stopped and stared.

"Well, well," said Mr. Grim. "I thought you was all crispy."

"Thomas would never do anything to hurt a Woolie," said Sarah. "Mr. Grim only wants to get rid of him because Thomas knows too much."

"She's a great one for putting the wrong words together, ain't she?" said Mr. Grim.

"Thomas knows what I know," said Sarah. "That it's perfectly safe in the Beyond."

Woolies gasped, and some even covered their ears.

"That's a pack of lies," said Mr. Grim.

"It's true," said Sarah. "The Beyond isn't scary. The Beyond won't hurt you—the Beyond can be a marvelous place."

"Never heard such poppycock," said Mr. Grim.

"A marvelous place with wonderful-wonderful grownups," continued Sarah. "Grownups who don't rant and rave, but who act proper and kind and take care of children. And the children in the Beyond sing songs and hop and twirl just to sing songs and hop and twirl—not because they're forced to slave away from dawn to dusk on crummy apples and cold mush."

"You think them Woolies is so mealy-brained they'd believe you?" scoffed Mr. Grim, growing increasingly red. "Ha! Everyone knows the Beyond is chock full of poison."

"It's full of fresh air," said Sarah, thrilled that the Woolies listened so intently. "And shady trees and whistling birds and lazy cats and twinkling stars and full moons and soft pillows and mashed potatoes and loving fathers and well-meaning aunts and—"

"Enough mumbo jumbo," cried Mr. Grim. "Nigel, fetch me the brat."

But Nigel seemed fascinated by Sarah's description of the outside world, and she thought that he didn't appear particularly anxious to quiet her. After a few halfhearted steps, he stopped to watch as Sarah dug in her pockets. She retrieved her woolen sling and Dee Dee's apple.

"Bleeding barnacle," muttered Mr. Grim.

Sarah loaded the apple into the sling and swung it over her head. A whirring noise grew as the weapon swung in faster and faster circles. Hoping that her aim had improved, Sarah grunted and fired the apple towards the ceiling.

SMASH!

Dazzling shafts of sunlight flooded through the cracks spidering across the frosted glass. Woolies shrank to the walls, but every nose pointed up and every eye forgot to blink.

"THAT POISON WILL TURN YOUR INNARDS TO GLOP!" shouted Mr. Grim, and the children crowded closer to the doors.

"It won't hurt you," cried Sarah. "That's honest-honest sunshine, and that's honest-honest blue sky."

"Don't listen to her," warned Mr. Grim. "I tell you it's poison!"

"Please, Freck," Sarah begged him. "You know the sun is harmless. Tell them!"

Freck shuffled forward and stopped next to the fine dust shimmering inside a sunbeam.

"Boy, you're making a big mistake," growled Mr. Grim. "Save yourself while you still can."

"Please, Freck," Sarah urged him. "Trust me."

Slowly, Freck extended his arm, opened his hand, and let his fingertips brush the sunbeam. The mouths of the other Woolies formed perfect soundless circles, but Freck smiled and stuck his palm in the brilliant light.

Seeing that Freck's hand didn't shrivel up, drop off, or explode in flames, several Woolies joined Freck and passed quick hands through the sunlight. But soon they let their arms linger, and they giggled as the warm sun danced over their bodies.

Bellowing more curses, Mr. Grim rumbled after Sarah and cut off her escape routes until she had nowhere to go. Nowhere except the wrong way. After three steps backward, Sarah felt her heels hanging over empty air.

"You cheeky little polecat," said Mr. Grim, inching forward with arms stretched wide. "I'm gonna skin your hide."

Teetering on the edge, Sarah turned to face the pit and did the unthinkable. She jumped. She knew she wasn't a bird, but she couldn't keep from fluttering her arms as she plunged into the pit.

CLUNK!

"Have you snapped your string?" cried Thomas as Sarah clutched the top of his swinging cage. "You should have stayed put."

"It's a little late for that," said Sarah. Growing dizzy as the cage spun on its rope, she tried not to look at the sharks below. Above, she heard the old man's mocking voice.

"Imagine," sneered Mr. Grim. "Today them no-leggers is

getting dessert as well." Sarah watched his scowl return as he peered over the side of the pit. "Why ain't that cage moving? Why ain't they dropping?"

Sarah heard Mr. Grim stomp away through scurrying Woolies, complaining, "Want anything done round here, you got to do it yourself."

The cage jerked into motion and resumed its slow fall. Holding on to the top with one hand, Sarah strained with her other hand to reach the door lock's iron pin. Her arm was too short.

"Whatever happens, Sarah, I'm grateful," said Thomas, clinging to the bamboo bars. "Thanks for trying."

"I'm still trying," groaned Sarah, lowering her leg over the side of the cage. Closer to the sharks, Sarah could see their cold lidless eyes. She looked away and gave the pin a hard kick.

Nothing.

"And I'm sorry I didn't tell you about the Beyond," said Thomas, speaking faster as they sank towards the seething waters.

"You were protecting the children," said Sarah, aiming another kick. Distracted by bits of earth crumbling from a section of the pit's wall, she missed the pin and almost flew into the water.

"I was wrong to be such a frown-maker," said Thomas as Sarah struggled to right herself atop the jiggling cage.

"You did what you considered best," said Sarah. She kicked the pin a third time, and it moved.

"AHHHHHH!"

Snapping jaws burst into the air, and Sarah felt the jolt of the cage hitting the water. She heard Thomas draw a sharp breath as she wound up and delivered one last mighty kick. The pin flew into the air, and the door swung open.

Thomas shrieked as a shark chomped through the bamboo floor as if it were nothing more than buttered bread. He scrambled out the door and scurried up the bamboo to join Sarah on top of the cage.

Sarah clutched Thomas and hung onto the cage's rope as earth rained from the pit's wall and splashed onto the thrashing sharks. Sinking towards the snarl of fins and tails, she saw row upon row of razor-sharp teeth.

A clump of dirt smacked off Sarah's ear.

"Hedgehogs in handkerchiefs!"

A small fist punched through the pit's wall, and a thin arm wriggled out. Another arm frantically pushed away more earth, and Dee Dee's button nose popped into view. The small Worm's fingernails clawed at the pit wall as an opening grew big enough for her head and shoulders. Sarah spotted more arms behind Dee Dee madly clearing more dirt.

Large clumps tumbled to the frenzied water, and Sarah and Thomas clung to the rope as the swarm of no-leggers chewed the bamboo into matchsticks. Sarah felt Thomas give her a boost and shinny up the rope behind her. Her white knuckles squeezed the swaying rope, and her palms blistered as she and Thomas shifted their bodies to swing the rope towards the wall, where Dee Dee stretched out an arm to catch them. Sarah brushed Dee Dee's fingers, but couldn't grab them. Other Worms clung to Dee Dee's legs so she could hang farther from the escape hole.

"AHHHHHHH!"

Thomas lost his grip and slid down the rope before snagging Sarah's foot. Sarah hugged the quivering rope while Thomas hoisted himself back up.

"Thomas!"

A shark leapt from the pit, snapping its jaws.

"Swing!" urged Thomas.

Sarah scrunched into her tummy and then flung out her chest, matching Thomas's rhythm as the rope swung in larger arcs. Her arms and shoulders smoldered with pain. At the lowest point of her swing, she caught a whiff of rancid fish breath and gazed into the gaping mouth of a shark.

Thomas kicked off the shark's nose for the extra momentum they needed to reach the wall. Sarah clamped on to Dee Dee's elbows. She felt the bunny girl's thin arms strain to pull her nearer. Sarah's wet hands slithered down Dee Dee's arms to her wrists, and she felt the girl's weight shift towards her. She was pulling Dee Dee into the pit!

"Let go," cried Sarah, releasing her own grip.

But Dee Dee squeezed Sarah's wrists even tighter and skidded on the dirt until half her body hung in the pit. Sarah watched Dee Dee grit her teeth and blink away sweat as the Worms behind her dug in their heels. The children furiously heaved on the girl's scrawny legs and slowly dragged Dee Dee back. Swaying closer, more arms snagged Sarah and yanked her into the hole. She collapsed in the dirt as Thomas scrambled past her onto a tangle of panting Worms.

Too weak to return Dee Dee's hug, Sarah gulped air as she spotted Nigel high above peering over the edge of the pit. Sarah thought she recognized a sigh of relief.

"You Woolies get this bloody pit covered up!" yelled Nigel. His eyes locked with Sarah's, and for a moment he didn't twitch.

MOONLIGHT
AT THE END
OF THE TUNNEL

DEEP IN the Worms' cave, beside the opening in the cliff wall, Sarah sat alone gazing out to sea. Unending skies of gray matched her mood.

Clink! Clink! Clink!

The sound of clinking metal triggered memories of her father's sword flashing as he fought off the pirates. If Father were here, he'd know what to do, thought Sarah, and then she sagged even more. But Father's not here and never will be.

Clink! Clink! Clink!

On the other side of the cave, the Worms leaned forward as Thomas used a rock to open a jumbo-sized tin of canned food. Sarah recognized the labelless tin from Mr. Grim's pantry.

The Worms took turns speculating what the day's mystery meal would be.

"Fish heads?"

"Pigs' knuckles?"

"Turkey necks?"

"It swishes around too much," said Thomas, shaking the tin.

Sarah hated to imagine what lurked inside the dented metal, but the Worms gleefully guessed.

"Jellied spinach?"

"Stewed tomatoes?"

"Creamed corn?"

"It's not that swishy," said Thomas, shifting the tin for another assault.

Clink! Clink! Clink!

Opening tins with a rock appeared to be an art. Thomas needed to bash the already dented metal hard enough to puncture the lid without spilling the precious food inside.

"Maybe it's glazed ham."

"Mmmmm."

Sarah decided that glazed ham was a crowd favorite.

Pppfff!

The rock pierced the tin, and the Worms sniffed the air for clues. "Well, it's not garlic cabbage," said Thomas, grinning. He used a stick to peel back the lid, and oohs and aahs rose from the appreciative diners. Sarah concluded that peaches in syrup were even more popular than glazed ham.

"Care for some supper?" asked Thomas, coming over with a bowl of the canned fruit.

"As long as I don't have to dangle on a rope to catch it," said Sarah.

"I'm sorry about that," said Thomas, reddening. "We've actually never been able to catch any fish, but the peaches are wonderful today."

Sarah accepted the peaches with a murmur of thanks and returned to staring out to sea as she ate. Thomas stood shifting his weight from foot to foot, until he gave his ear a very Nigel-like scratch and then sat next to her on the smooth rock floor.

"Poor Freck must think we're dead," he said.

Choked with guilt, Sarah only nodded and prayed that Freck had avoided any punishment for touching the sunbeam. She finished her five peach slices and was yearning for twenty-five more, when Dee Dee shyly approached.

"I can't eat all mine," said the little girl, offering her bowl to Sarah.

"Dee Dee, you'll be hungry later on," said Thomas.

"There's no room in my tummy."

"Finish your peaches," said Thomas in a sterner tone. "Or I'll make you eat twice as many turnips."

Judging by the way that Dee Dee gobbled her peach slices, slurped the juice from her bowl, and licked each one of her fingers dry, it was obvious that having a full stomach had been a white lie. Sarah realized that the girl had only wanted to share her meal.

"Dee Dee is a very pretty name," said Sarah.

"It's short for Defective and Deficient," explained Dee Dee.

"But that's horrible," said Sarah. "Who would call you such a spiteful thing?"

"Master Grim names all the Woolies," said Thomas.

"He's not our master anymore," said Sarah. "And she is certainly neither defective nor deficient."

"Oh, but I am," said Dee Dee. "Four lots of puny-news grew big, and I still stayed a spindle."

"Spindles are Woolies who stand in one spot while the others wind string around them," explained Thomas. "They become the flower centers."

"Well, I'm sure Dee Dee was a splendid flower center."

"Not really," admitted Dee Dee.

"And then she got too old," added Thomas. "At Dee Dee's age she should have been a Tweener."

"But I got too dizzy," said Dee Dee.

"I can imagine twirling about isn't for everyone," said Sarah.

"Master Grim tossed me from Woolie World after I unswallowed."

"Unswallowed?"

"Master Grim called it spewing," said Dee Dee.

"Dee Dee, it wasn't so bad," said Thomas. "Glop looks pretty much the same coming up as it does going down."

"Oh," said Sarah, not needing any more details. "Well, I'll continue to call you Dee Dee only because I think you're doubly 'Dee' lightful."

Dee Dee turned red and happily trotted away.

Thomas pointed out some of the other unfortunately named children: an undersized boy was called Flea not because of his size, but because Mr. Grim thought he was such a pest. The slowest-moving Worm was named Filler because Mr. Grim said the boy did nothing but take up space. No explanation was needed for the names Useless, Worthless, and Hopeless. Mercifully, most children were known by shorter versions of their names: Half for Half-wit; Stu for Stupid; and while Missy might sound like a girl's name, it was actually short for Mistake. Mr. Grim had concluded that kidnapping a color-blind boy to work in a rug factory was a definite mistake.

Sarah wondered, "How did you come by such a common name as Thomas?"

"Common," said Thomas with a laugh. "I'm the only Thomas on the whole island. There's nothing the same-same about my name. If you want a common name, you should really talk about Another One."

"Another One?"

"Master Grim can get lazy if he's naming more than one baby at a time," explained Thomas. "There's one Another One working in the nursery, another Another One working as a color bug, and three more Another Ones caring for the puny-news."

"Five children all named Another One?" marveled Sarah, and she licked traces of peach juice from her fingertips while she again adjusted her thinking to match her new surroundings.

⚓

That night, crammed under six woolen blankets and too tired for dreams, Sarah slept like a January bear. She only woke when the sun flooded into the cave. Considering that her mattress was hard rock, Sarah felt surprisingly well rested.

"Welcome to tomorrow," said Dee Dee, painfully shy as always.

"Good morning," said Sarah, stretching and yawning. She spotted other Worms tending a coal fire and taking turns shaking another large unlabeled tin. "What are today's guesses?"

"Flea guessed peaches again," said Dee Dee. "But he's just wishing."

"Well, I'm wishing for hot biscuits and some of Nigel's marmalade," said Sarah, rolling from bed.

Dee Dee helped Sarah fold her blankets as a stooped-over Thomas emerged from a small tunnel. Thomas paused to straighten his back and brush the coal dust from his Woolie suit.

"Good morning, Thomas," said Sarah.

"Cheeks high," said Thomas with a smile. "Dee Dee, would you please make sure the others are bubble scrubbed for swallow time?"

As Dee Dee scooted away, Thomas's face turned gloomy, and he swatted the coal dust a little harder.

"What's wrong?" asked Sarah.

"There's a new padlock on the door by the manure pile."

"You went back?"

"I wanted to snitch a few tins," said Thomas. "We've only got the one left."

"I know of a door to the storage room," said Sarah.

"Locked up tight."

"Oh dear," said Sarah. "We'll starve to death!"

"We'll be fine," said Thomas. "This morning will be our last guessing game for a while, that's all."

After washing in a basin, Sarah and Thomas watched the Worms happily feast on the last tin of canned food. A girl named Good for Nothing had correctly guessed that breakfast would be sugared yams.

The Worms spent the early morning in the abandoned

tunnels collecting stray bits of coal for the fire, and as with most Worm activities, they turned it into a game. Who could find the most lumps? Who could find the biggest lump? Who could find the oddest-shaped lump? Sarah scurried about like a clumsy gopher on a leash, but she preferred a rope around her waist to getting lost in the underground maze.

The next part of the day, Sarah and the Worms ventured aboveground to pick raspberries. The other Worms strolled unruffled among the thorny brambles, but Sarah's stinging scratches soon numbered more than her plucked berries.

She was grateful when Thomas asked her to help him find wild carrots and other edible roots in an open field. She quickly discovered that digging vegetables had its downside as well. Dirt burrowed under her fingernails, and the scorching sun baked her skin.

Heavenly seemed too mild a description for how Sarah felt when, after several hours, the children trekked to an icy stream for a drink and a dip. The Worms frolicked in the refreshing waters all the way down to the shore.

Thomas worried that Mr. Grim might discover Worm footprints on the beach, so he taught the children to cover their tracks by dragging branches behind them. Sarah towed the limb of a pine tree as she scavenged for seashells that would make good drinking cups.

Dee Dee was the first to stumble upon the mound of stones topped by a wooden cross. "What does it say?" she whispered, unable to read the inscription carved into the cross.

"'God bless my daughter,'" read Sarah, her voice numb and distant. "'Sarah Tufts—Lost at Sea.'" Though Sarah's eyes were rimmed with tears, she forced a smile. "They did a lovely job."

"A wonderful-wonderful job," agreed Dee Dee, and she slipped her hand into Sarah's. "But you're not lost. You're one of us now."

That night in the cave, after a meal of berries and small, crooked carrots, Sarah snuggled under her blankets and watched the sun drop past the horizon. Dee Dee's words played over in her head. Staring into the darkness, she realized that the little girl was right; Sarah could no longer pretend to be merely a visitor.

"I'm a Worm," she whispered to no one. "And a Worm hasn't time to mope around feeling sorry for herself."

The next day Sarah rose early and slipped out of the cave before any of the other Worms had even stirred. The morning sun found her crouched knee-deep in the ocean trying to catch a fish with her bare hands.

Waiting motionlessly (Aunt Margaret would have been proud of her self-control), Sarah focused on one of the curious fish that circled her. When it finally swam close enough, Sarah silently counted to three and lunged.

She clapped up great splashes and spit mouthfuls of salt water, but any fish within miles had been scared away.

Before anyone noticed her missing, Sarah dried off and joined the Worms for morning swallow time. After more raspberries and wild carrots, Sarah and the children went scavenging in the tunnels for coal. She laughed when Dee Dee excitedly revealed her find—a lump of coal shaped like a bullfrog.

Aboveground, Sarah and Thomas searched for anything edible as they strolled across a field of wildflowers. Thomas was describing how the bursts of living color inspired rug designs, when the earth beneath Sarah dissolved. Her feet broke through the dirt, and her legs disappeared up to her knees. Sarah's sudden decline in height didn't seem to surprise Thomas. Helping to free her, he explained that no one ever became too alarmed when the ground collapsed on an island with so many tunnels.

That afternoon, Thomas showed everyone how to hunt soldier crabs in the shallow water. Being the strongest, Thomas tilted the rocks, and the children scurried to catch the bright blue animals before they corkscrewed under the sand. Sarah quickly figured out how to pick up a crab without being pinched. Many red-fingered, shrieking Worms were slower to learn the same lesson.

That evening, the Worms watched suspiciously as the creatures boiled in an old pot, but twenty minutes later everyone laughed and chattered and devoured the scrumptious white meat. Huddled around the fire, several Worms nudged Dee Dee, whispering to the small girl while throwing glances at Sarah. After more prodding, Dee Dee approached Sarah.

"You've been beyond the Beyond?" asked Dee Dee. "Honest-honest?"

"If you mean, have I been across the ocean," said Sarah, "the answer is yes—honest-honest."

"And full up nice grownups live beyond the Beyond?" asked Dee Dee. The Worms behind her leaned in and listened hard.

Remembering Thomas's annoyance at a similar discussion with Freck, Sarah looked for his reaction.

"I guess it can't hurt," Thomas said with a shrug. "We've already been tossed out of Woolie World."

"Of course," Sarah answered Dee Dee. "Beyond the Beyond live plenty of nice grownups."

Upon hearing such a fantastic claim, all the children spoke at once: What do they look like? Do they live in tunnels? What do they eat? And each of Sarah's answers prompted twenty more questions—many of the same questions Sarah had asked her father when she was younger. The Worms never tired of hearing about life beyond the Beyond. They were amazed by the idea of homes and front parlors and teatime and pie forks. They were flabbergasted by the notion of Christmas and Easter and other holidays when you didn't have to do a stitch of work all day. And they were totally confused by triple-layered chocolate cake, but Sarah knew that even a university professor couldn't describe the taste of chocolate to a boy who hadn't already felt it melt on his tongue.

Stubbornly, Sarah continued to rise each morning with the sun and go alone to the shore where she would wade into the surf and try to catch a fish. Returning empty-handed, Sarah would spend the rest of the day with the other Worms, gathering coal and foraging for food. Thomas proved helpful in teaching Sarah how to pick raspberries without bleeding to death. He showed her how to weave flowers and grass into sun hats, and how to dig for turtle eggs. Thomas impressed her most by figuring out all these things on his own with nothing more than heaps of common sense. She felt sure that Thomas was smarter than many folks who had read complete encyclopedias.

Supper around the fire and stories of beyond the Beyond took up most evenings until it was time to sleep. Days and nights blurred together with the same routine. Being a Worm wasn't glamorous, but Sarah enjoyed her new friends and soon settled into life on the island.

On several of her morning fishing trips, Sarah got near enough to touch a tail or fin before it slipped through her fingers. Seeing a fish race away only made her more determined.

Finally, after two weeks of early rising, Sarah stood stone-still in the ocean while a fish explored the back of her knee. Hoping the fish was both curious and slow, Sarah waited for it to swim to the front of her leg.

Thwack!

Sarah's hands cut through the water, and she scooped the fish to the surface—juggling it in midair as she hurried to shore. Only when her catch wiggled safely on dry land did Sarah squeal with delight.

That night, Sarah beamed with pride as everyone feasted on her fish.

Still, thoughts of her father were never far away, and as the coal fire died and darkness crept into the cave, sadness crowded out her joy. While everyone else slept, Sarah stood by the opening in the cliff wall and gazed out at the night sky. A low moon shone bright and cheery, but Sarah knew the truth—the moon didn't really shine on its own. It only reflected the sun's rays. Sarah didn't see how she could go on pretending to be bright and cheery without her father. Like the moon, Sarah felt like a big pretender.

Returning to her spot among the sleeping Worms, Sarah saw that Dee Dee had kicked off her covers. "At least one of us should be cozy-snug," whispered Sarah as she gently tucked the blankets around the small child.

MERMAIDS
AND GORILLAS

"PLEASE, FLEA, just try one," said Sarah, coaxing the boy to eat his lunch of wild turnips.

"They fight with my tongue," said Flea, turning away from the bitter root.

"You need vegetables to grow tall and strong," said Sarah. "You want big muscles like Thomas, don't you?"

"Won't berries make muscles?" asked Flea.

"Berries are good," agreed Sarah, "but Father always said, 'You can't run on one leg.'"

"May I hear another Father story?" said Flea. "Please?" Father stories were a favorite among the Worms.

"Father was—," Sarah began before correcting herself. "Father *is* a very wise man who taught me that if you eat turnips every once in a while, you'll appreciate how delicious carrots are."

Flea selected the smallest bit of turnip he could find and cautiously placed it in his mouth. After almost thirty seconds of slow-motion chewing, he swallowed the morsel as if it were an entire bushel.

"Giraffes and geraniums!" Sarah jumped back and pointed at Flea's foot. "Did you see that? I think one of your toes just grew."

"Really?" asked an astounded Flea.

"You'd better make sure those other toes get some turnip," said Sarah. "Unless you want lopsided feet."

"Of course not," said Flea, selecting another piece of turnip and chewing more energetically.

Satisfied, Sarah sat back and enjoyed a breeze wafting through the opening in the cliff wall. Something among the sea's distant waves caught her eye, and she sprang to her feet.

"LOOK! LOOK! LOOK!" There was no mistaking it— a scruffy cargo ship was sailing directly towards the island. "HELLO! HELLO! OVER HERE! HELP!" whooped Sarah, bouncing about and waving her arms.

"Shhh," warned Thomas, pulling Sarah from the opening. "Last thing you want is them thugs coming around here."

"How do you know they're thugs?"

"Because they are."

"But, but, you could be mistaken," said Sarah. "Perhaps they're good and friendly."

"They aren't good or friendly," said Thomas. "They work for Master Grim. Twice a year they haul away the done rugs, and they'd just as soon slit your throat as say hello."

Sarah slumped back to her seat. "Doesn't anyone nice ever stop by?"

"Look, Sarah," said Flea, flipping his empty turnip bowl upside down. "I ate every one."

"That's very good, Flea," said Sarah, summoning a smile for the proud child.

"Look how big my toes are," said Flea.

"I'll sneak you on board," declared Thomas.

"I beg your pardon?"

"The ship—I'll sneak you on board the ship," explained Thomas. "I'll hide you in a rug, and they'll put you on the ship, and when you get to market, you can make a run for it."

"Roll me up in a rug?" said Sarah.

"Chances are they'd never see you among hundreds of other rugs," said Thomas.

"That's a brilliant idea," said Sarah.

"We'll make sure you've got enough food," said Thomas.

"That's a fabulous idea."

"And plenty of water."

"That's a fantastic idea."

"So we'll sneak you on board tonight."

"No," said Sarah.

"What?"

"Definitely not."

"I thought it was a brilliant fabulous fantastic idea?" said Thomas.

"Oh, it is," said Sarah. "It's even wonderful-wonderful, but the only way I'm leaving this island is with everyone else— Worms and Woolies."

"But, Sarah, the Worms and Woolies have never been off this island," reasoned Thomas. "They don't know any better."

"We're sticking together," said Sarah, crossing her arms.

"Beyond the Beyond is just a bedtime story to them!" said Thomas.

"We're sticking together."

"They've got no one out there to miss."

"Well, if you weren't so silly," said Sarah, "you might realize that I'd miss them, and maybe I'd even miss you."

⚓

Meanwhile, far from the scruffy cargo ship entering the harbor of Coal Island, another ship sailed the open sea. On the deck of the *London Gorilla,* Bear mended his mustard-and-cherry-striped tights while Black Tooth lounged in a hammock, balancing his dinner plate on his belly as he gnawed the gristle from a carcass of small bones. "Mmmm, this is the life," said Black Tooth, squeezing one eye and farting.

"SHIP OFF THE PORT BOW!" bawled Stinger from his perch high in the crow's-nest. "SHIP OFF THE PORT BOW!"

Bear put down his sewing and looked seaward through his spyglass. "Cap'n, Cap'n, it's that Lordship's ship—whoooa!"

Stepping backward, Bear tripped over Black Tooth's hammock and sent his captain's plate flying.

"You bleedin' idiot," growled Black Tooth, wrestling himself from the hammock.

"Sorry, sorry, sorry," pleaded Bear. On hands and knees he spied the tiny skeleton scattered near his captain's plate. "Them ain't fish bones. I thought Cook said we's having bluegill goulash?"

"That's what you lot is having," said Black Tooth. "Wasn't enough of this one to go around."

"This one?"

"Him," said Black Tooth with a nod towards his cabin door.

Bear cupped his ear to listen for parrot noises. Silence. "Holy halibut!"

"The scurvy thing tasted a far sight better than he squawked."

"But the bird was your matey," moaned Bear as he tenderly collected the delicate bones.

"Forget the bird," said Black Tooth. "What'd you see?"

"It's the Lordship's ship for sure."

"I don't care what Pa says about leaving stinking royalty alone," snarled Black Tooth. "I'm gonna squash that pest."

"How?" asked Bear. "Last time he whomped you."

Black Tooth kicked Bear's backside and sent the parrot bones flying again. Bear folded up to protect against another boot, but Black Tooth snatched the spyglass and marched to the railing. "That was last time," said Black Tooth, squinting through the lens. "This time I got meself a plan."

⚓

From the deck of the *Shy Mermaid,* Captain Murphy surveyed the pirate ship through his telescope. The *London Gorilla*'s canvas hung slack, and the ship bobbed gently on the water. Black Tooth stood alone at the railing waving a white flag of surrender. Captain Murphy felt the pink rush to his cheeks. "Are we to honestly trust the foul dog?"

Lord Tufts's voice sounded composed, but muscles flexed in his jaw. "We must respect maritime rules."

"But, M'Lord—"

"Black Tooth's contempt for the law gives us no cause to behave as barbarians."

Captain Murphy continued to fidget and grind his teeth as the two ships grew closer and closer. From thirty yards away, Black Tooth appeared to be the only pirate on deck. "You know, M'Lord, book justice ain't always the best way. I'm just saying, if anything should happen to go wrong, it's a long walk home."

"Steady, Captain," said Lord Tufts.

"AHOY, YOUR LORDSHIP," Black Tooth called out across the water. "CAN'T WE PUT THIS NASTINESS BEHIND US?"

"DO YOU ACKNOWLEDGE YOUR CRIMES?" asked Lord Tufts.

"REGRETTABLY," admitted the pirate captain. "AND NOW I'M HOPIN' TO MAKE AMENDS." Black Tooth lowered his head like a meek schoolboy, but his rotten teeth flashed a dark smile.

"Lord have mercy!" muttered Captain Murphy as the pirate crew sprang above the starboard railing. Amid their whooping and hollering, three gunports swung open, and cannon muzzles flashed red.

KABOOM! KABOOM! KABOOM!

The iron balls splintered the *Shy Mermaid*'s hull, and Captain Murphy tasted blood as he crashed off the railing. Sprawled on his back, dust and smoke settled about him, and he heard the roar of the ocean gushing into his ship. On hands and knees, Lord Tufts groped his way to Captain Murphy, and they helped gather each other off the heaving deck.

"MAN YOUR STATIONS!" ordered Captain Murphy, spitting red. His crew wobbled to the cannons, but the pirates had already reloaded.

KABOOM! KABOOM! KABOOM!

Hot iron sliced through a sailor's leg, and Lord Tufts jumped to take the screaming man's place. While the ship tilted and water swept into the main hold, Lord Tufts rammed a powder keg down the cannon muzzle and lit the fuse.

KABOOM!

The *Shy Mermaid* was sinking fast, but still on a collision course with the *London Gorilla.* Captain Murphy shouted over the chaos, "READY THE GRAPPLING HOOKS."

KABOOM! KABOOM!

MISSING EARS
AND FINDING KEYS

NIGEL NEVER enjoyed this part of the job. The crew from the cargo ship always frowned at the mounds and mounds of new rugs filling the done room. Uneasy on dry land at the best of times, the eight sailors appeared extra cranky around such cheery colors.

"I don't see why we gotta muck about in the middle of the night," complained Three O'Clock, fingering the scar that slashed his cheek and nose like the hands of a timepiece.

"We can't have children seeing strangers from the Beyond," explained Nigel, stroking his mustache and hoping he sounded like part of the management.

"Codswallop!" said Three O'Clock. "It's ridiculous to be traipsing about a harbor in the pitch black." The other sailors grunted their agreement as they picked their teeth and scratched various body parts.

"It's the way we've always done it," said Nigel, bouncing on the balls of his feet to gain some height.

"And I'm telling you it's ridiculous."

"If it bothers you so much," said Nigel, "why not tell Master Grim to kiss your sweet backside?" Nigel smiled to himself as the other sailors shuffled farther from Three O'Clock and softened their glares.

Three O'Clock hemmed and hawed. "It'd be easier in the morning, that's all." But Nigel knew that Three O'Clock, like every sailor in the room, would rather share his bath with a family of tomcats than challenge Mr. Grim.

⚓

Meanwhile, deep within the earth, Sarah and the Worms were following Thomas through a tunnel. Sarah brandished a broken broom handle while others carried sticks and sharp rocks. Thomas paced off his steps, chanting, "105, 106, 107 . . ." At 108 he stopped.

"You're sure?" asked Sarah.

"Sure I'm sure," said Thomas. "Fairly sure." He used his stick to scratch an X on the tunnel's dirt ceiling. Then he began chipping away at the hard earth. The taller Worms helped dig as the rest of the Worms cleared the dirt that fell.

Within minutes the hole was too high for anyone to reach, so Thomas crouched down, and Sarah climbed up his back. He held her legs as she sat on his shoulders and dug. When the hole was beyond the reach of Sarah's broken broom, Dee Dee gave Flea a boost, and he scrambled up Thomas's and Sarah's backs. Sarah held the boy's feet as he sat on her shoulders and continued upwards digging. When the stack of children grew to four—Dee Dee on top of Flea on top of Sarah on top of Thomas—Sarah felt as if she were part of a circus act.

⚓

Back in the done room, Nigel leaned against one of the wagons that the sailors had loaded with the new rugs. "Slow down," he whined as Three O'Clock tossed another rug onto the wagon's swelling pile. "I'll never be able to move the bloomin' thing."

"You wanna cart 'em out one at a time?" asked Three O'Clock. "It'd take all bloody year."

"But at year's end I'd still have my back," said Nigel.

⚓

Thomas crawled up through the hole and turned back to grab Sarah's hand. His strength startled her as she lurched to the surface and scrambled onto the grass.

"Sorry," she whispered, banging into two drowsy sheep.

Sarah shook the dirt from her hair and helped the rest of

the Worms clamber up to the field of living string. Skittish to be back inside Woolie World, the Worms crouched low to mingle with the flock. The few four-leggers still awake looked once and became bored. Sarah counted the last Worm popping from the hole and gave Thomas a thumbs-up. He herded the Worms through the sheep and out the doors. Running her hand along the shaggy walls and hustling over the soft springy carpet, Sarah followed a long line down the hallways.

Like Sarah, the other children's swiveling heads and darting eyes caught every flutter of wool. The same dread must have itched at every child—would Master Grim be lurking around the next corner? Up ahead, Thomas stopped, and the children bumped together.

"What is it?" whispered Sarah. "Why are we stopping?"

Thomas nodded at the shiny padlock on the nursery door. "It's the same as the new lock on the door by the manure—"

A faint squeaking noise interrupted Thomas. Sarah held her breath and through the squeaking heard the indistinguishable rumblings of a conversation. She recognized Nigel's voice, but the other man sounded nothing like Mr. Grim. Whoever they were, they were getting closer. With no place to hide, a buzz of terror traveled through the Worms.

"Shhh," urged Thomas.

The squeaking grew louder.

⚓

Flushed and grimacing, Nigel pushed a squeaky wagon overflowing with rugs. The thick-limbed sailor beside him could have been pushing a feather for all the effort that showed on his face.

Turning the wagon into the nursery hallway, Nigel groaned as the pain burned hotter. "There's plenty more wagons to bust a gut on," he said, stopping to rub his back. "No sense rushing things."

"Huh?" said Huh. (His crew mates had called him "Huh" ever since his ear had been chewed off in a bar fight.)

"I need a break," said Nigel.

"Anita who?"

"I NEED A BREAK," yelled Nigel, and he flopped onto the carpet with more groaning.

"We just started," said Huh.

"Just give me a minute," sighed Nigel, stretching out his back.

"Huh?"

"I need a min—"

Wiggling yarn in the rafters overhead sidetracked Nigel. He blinked twice. The yarn hung perfectly still.

"Anita who?" Huh asked again.

Nigel stared harder into the shadows. Nothing.

"You finally met a woman?" said Huh.

Puzzled, Nigel surveyed the empty hallway and the nursery door and its new lock.

"Well, if them rugs ain't going nowhere, neither am I," decided Huh, and he started to sit.

"No, you're right," yelled Nigel, leaping to his feet and tugging at Huh. "We just started, and it's time for work. How about I take care of this wagon and you go back to the done room for another?"

"Huh?"

"I SAID I'LL TAKE THIS WAGON—"

"Oh, I heard you," said Huh. "I just can't figure out if you're plain batty or raving mad."

"I got a second wind," yelled Nigel, using all his strength to get the squeaky load of rugs moving. "Besides, we ain't got all bloody night."

As Nigel rolled away down the hall, he heard Huh calling, "You're an odd duck. I wonder what Anita sees in you!"

⚓

When both men had disappeared, Thomas poked his head from the shaggy rafters. "Clear," he said, and Sarah and the other Worms dropped to the soft carpet.

Moments later, the double doors to the Woolies' dormitory opened just enough for the Worms to slip inside. The room was tranquil except for the rumbling snores of Mr. Grim asleep in his chair. Crawling on their stomachs, the Worms spread out and began silently waking the Woolies.

Sarah gently nudged Freck, but the boy only rolled over and pulled his blanket tighter. "Freck, wake up," she whispered, nudging him a second time. "It's me."

Freck's eyes flickered open. Seeing Sarah, he nearly jumped out of his Woolie suit before she held him down and gave him the hush sign.

"I thought you were doing the forever blink in a no-legger's belly," he whispered, hugging her tight.

"Sorry about giving you such a scare," said Sarah. "But my lids are still moving, and my bottom half has as many legs as ever."

"What about Thomas?" Freck asked.

"Cheeks up," said Sarah with a nod towards Thomas, who was rousing more Woolies.

But Freck didn't smile. "I'm sorry, Sarah, your string was a tangle, and I quick-footed the other way—"

"Shhh, no more of that," said Sarah. "You're plenty brave."

Everything proceeded smoothly as sleepy Woolies left their blankets one at a time and the Worms ushered them out the doors.

"Where are you going?" asked Sarah, grabbing Thomas by the elbow as he crawled past in the opposite direction.

"I still need the nursery key from Master Grim's pocket," whispered Thomas.

"No," insisted Sarah. "My hands are smaller."

"But—"

"No buts," said Sarah stubbornly.

Thomas hesitated before conceding. "Be careful."

As Sarah reached Mr. Grim snoozing in his chair, she thought it a miracle that he could sleep at all with such a racket of snorting and wind-sucking. Mr. Grim's whistling nose hairs and the dribble of drool leaking from his mouth distracted Sarah from her own fear. She braced herself and slowly reached for Mr. Grim's vest pocket.

Mr. Grim squirmed, and Sarah froze. When he settled, she carefully slipped her hand into the pocket. Only a watch. She slid her hand into his jacket pocket. A few coins. She slid her hand into his right pants pocket.

Mr. Grim's body shifted, pinning Sarah's hand against the chair. Sarah peered up at his fluttering nose hairs and waited for Mr. Grim's next spasm. When he shifted, she dug deeper into the pocket and hit something metal. Clutching the object, Sarah slowly withdrew her hand and grinned; it only made sense that one of the shiny new keys attached to the chain would open the shiny new padlock on the nursery door.

Sarah held her breath as she inched out more of the key

chain. After two feet she still hadn't seen its end. She crawled back, and another twelve inches of links emerged from Mr. Grim's pocket. Then the key chain drew tight as if snagged on something.

Sarah tugged gently on the chain, but it wouldn't budge. A slightly stronger tug also failed to free the key chain. Sarah yanked harder at the same moment Mr. Grim snorted and rolled the opposite way. The key chain jerked from her hand.

"OWWWW!"

The metal whip snapped back into Mr. Grim's nose, and he clambered from his chair. Panic-stricken, Sarah remained kneeling in plain view.

NEW GHOST
AND
SAME OLD BOGEYMAN

"LORD HAVE mercy!" gasped Mr. Grim as the blood drained from his face. "She's come back from the dead!"

After a heartbeat of hesitation, Sarah confidently stood and spread her arms. "Woooooo, wooooo," she said, swaying her body and fluttering her hands. "I am the ghost of Sarah Tufts. Woooo woooo." Sarah wasn't sure what "woo woo" meant, but she thought it sounded like something a returning spirit might say; at least Mr. Grim seemed convinced.

"Please, please," Mr. Grim begged. "I never meant no harm."

"Woo woo," said Sarah, stalling for time while she figured out her escape. "You've been a very bad man—a frown-maker."

"But I'm gonna change all that," said Mr. Grim. "I'm gonna change everything about me."

"You must treat people nicer," said Sarah.

"I will—I will," sniveled Mr. Grim. "I swear it."

"And you must be a better father," said Sarah, swishing her arms about.

"I promise," cried Mr. Grim. "Don't hurt me and I'll be the best pa there ever was."

Wanting to be the best ghost there ever was, Sarah reeled forward. "Wooo—ouch!"

Sarah slipped on a blanket, stubbed her toe on the chair, and landed on her rear end. Looking up at Mr. Grim's narrowing eyes, she stopped clutching her foot and flapped a feeble "Woo woo."

"Since when do banshees stub their toes?" snarled Mr. Grim. "You ain't no stinking ghost."

"Would you believe I'm a bad dream?" asked Sarah.

Mr. Grim looked over Sarah's head and shouted, "YOU THERE, STOP!"

Scrambling to her feet, Sarah spotted a Woolie crawling towards the door and shouted even louder, "RUN!"

Woolies and Worms scattered like mice as Mr. Grim charged after Sarah bellowing, "You'll be a ghost soon enough when I wring your neck!" Zigzagging across the room, she eluded Mr. Grim's grasp until the last child had darted safely out the doors.

"Porcupines and pincushions!" squeaked Sarah as Mr. Grim

snagged a fistful of her hair. She grit her teeth and danced on tiptoes, holding tight to Mr. Grim's forearm.

"Should've cracked your skull the moment I laid eyes on you," hissed Mr. Grim. Thousands of stinging hair roots sucked away Sarah's voice. "But I won't make the mistake of waiting again—AHHHHH!"

At that moment Thomas kicked Mr. Grim so hard that the old man pitched Sarah away from him and clutched his own ankle. Sarah dropped to the carpet and scampered off like a four-legger.

"You'll pay for that, boy," cried Mr. Grim, hopping after Thomas.

The last thing Sarah glimpsed before she flew out the door was Thomas whirling across the dormitory flinging blankets at Mr. Grim.

Sarah zipped down the empty hallway, breathing so hard that she almost missed Dee Dee's tiny voice. "Sarah," whispered Dee Dee, waiting halfway inside the doors to the weave room. "Sarah, in here."

Sarah thought it would be much safer to flee Woolie World altogether, but she let Dee Dee tug her inside. Seeing every single Woolie and Worm skittering about the weave room, Sarah went from uncomfortable to baffled. Why had Freck just run past with an armful of yarn?

"Dee Dee, why aren't they at the tunnel?" asked Sarah.

"Corners up, Sarah," Dee Dee assured her. "You and me will just be standing spindle stiff."

"This is no time for flowers and rug weaving!" cried Sarah. "Why are we stopping?"

"Because I told them to," gasped Thomas, rushing inside to join the crowd.

"Where's Mr. Grim?" asked Sarah.

"He's gone off screaming and flapping to the done room," panted Thomas, and before Sarah could urge him to get the children to the tunnel, Thomas faced the Woolies and gave the order. "READY THE PIT!"

Sarah's jaw dropped. "Are you mad?"

⚓

Mr. Grim stormed into the done room and found the cargo ship crew lolling about when they should have been loading the rugs on wagons. "MOVE YOUR ARSES AND FETCH ME THEM WRETCHED BRATS."

"Rats?" asked Huh, turning in a circle as he checked the area for rodents.

"Brats!" seethed Mr. Grim. "Them cursed Woolies! Round up every last one of them."

"Woolies ain't part of our deal," complained Three O'Clock. "We gets paid for moving rugs not bleeding baby-sitting."

"Then I'll triple your bleeding pay," growled Mr. Grim, and he stepped aside as Three O'Clock scrambled past Huh to be the first one out the door.

⚓

In the weave room, heaps and heaps of yarn formed a perfect square as if in preparation for the weaving of another rug. But Sarah knew why no other children joined her on the carpet at the center of the square. She carefully kept her feet in one spot and strained with her toes to feel the hard plank beneath the soft yarn. At the same time, she tried not to think about the scaly beasts lurking in the hidden pit below.

Sarah concentrated on the square's edge twelve feet away and her target—a six-inch splash of charcoal gray yarn flecked with silver. All she would have to do is walk in a perfectly straight line for twelve feet and she would be standing directly on the patch of charcoal and silver. It would be simple enough to do, if she just didn't think of the sharks in the cold black water below.

"It's called squeezed-eye gray," explained Freck, speaking loudly enough to be heard from the square's edge. "On account of those sparkly bits you get when you lock your lids." The color did remind Sarah of the tiny specks of light that played on the backs of her eyelids.

"Let's hope it's a lucky color," said Sarah, shuddering at the thought of missing her mark. Freck's nervous smile didn't help, and neither did all the worried faces crowded along the edge. Again, Sarah tried to ignore thoughts of the hungry you-know-whats swimming you-know-where.

She heard Thomas instruct the sniffling milkweed girl and several beet boys from the color room. "Fetch your slings and anything you can zing, and meet us at the color bug vats," he told them. "And keep your lids open."

The children nodded their understanding, and Sarah heard the milkweed girl's excited chatter as she and the beet boys raced out the side exit.

"I should be the one doing it," said Thomas, turning to Sarah. "It's too dangerous."

"Thomas, it's all feet on the flat," said Sarah, hoping she sounded more certain than she felt. "Besides, it's my neck he wants to wring the most."

"Cheeks high," said Thomas. "And remember, just—"

"Just run straight for the squeezed-eye gray," said Sarah. "Thomas, I'll be fine. Freck, tell him I'll be fine."

Freck nodded. "All she has to do is not think about the no-leggers."

"Freck!"

A split-second image of grinning shark teeth fled Sarah's mind as the weave room doors swung open with a loud *crash*. The crew of the cargo ship barged inside, and Sarah gulped down her urge to run. Scarred faces and missing ears unsettled her, but she tried to calm herself as Mr. Grim bulled his way to the front of the eight thugs.

Sarah wondered if the crew even knew how greasy and disheveled they appeared. She found herself borrowing one of Aunt Margaret's questions, "What class of fool waltzes about in public looking like that?" Perhaps, she thought, the sailors had thrown all their mirrors into the sea at the same time they rid their ship of all brushes. Not a single hair on a single head had ever been smoothed by a comb.

The sailors wore a collection of dirty shirts and dirtier pants. Sarah had a strong inkling that the scowling sailors feared only one thing—soap.

"Nine grown men to gather up a few children?" said Sarah, tsk-tsking in her best Aunt Margaret imitation. "You're certainly a sad lot."

"Fetch me every last one of them sneaky brats," snarled Mr. Grim, and the eight sailors barreled towards Sarah.

The children's shrieking drowned out the rest of Mr. Grim's threats as Sarah carefully turned in place and walked straight for the patch of squeezed-eye gray. Eight feet from her target, she heard the raspy howls of the sailors. Six feet from the edge, she prayed that nothing had shifted below her toes. Four feet from—

Sarah's foot slipped, and she felt the edge of the plank beneath the carpet. Her wobble made the children gasp, but her momentum kept her moving forward and she corrected her route. Nimbly, she stepped onto the patch of squeezed-eye gray and skittered across a mound of butterscotch yarn to topple into Freck's arms.

Sarah rolled over on solid ground to watch a row of sailors reach the far edge of the square. Six men trampled over the piles of string and rushed forward.

For a moment it appeared that the surprised men were running on air as the planks disappeared beneath their feet. Then the carpet buckled and pulled free of its edges, and in the next instant, it had swallowed up the wailing men and plunged into the pit. In the next instant, the carpet snapped tight—still attached to two diagonal corners—and hung like a twisted-up hammock. Sarah could see the outlines of writhing sailors in the giant snare suspended above the frenzied sharks.

The two sailors behind the first wave, the scar-faced man and the man missing an ear, didn't stop quickly enough. They skidded through piles of string, slipped over the edge, and clung from the rim of the pit. Miraculously, Mr. Grim stood teetering where Sarah had stood—atop the lone plank that spanned the shark pit. Beneath Mr. Grim, a shirtless sailor hugged the plank and blubbered. His dangling legs wriggled and squirmed.

"You're shaking it too much," cried Mr. Grim, walking on the sailor's fingers. Sarah and the children shrieked louder than the man who dropped towards the swirl of scaly no-leggers and slammed crotch first onto the hanging carpet.

"Follow me!" yelled Thomas, quick-stepping for the side exit.

But Sarah stood spindle stiff as she watched the scar-faced and the earless sailors struggle up to the surface. Only the sight of Mr. Grim gingerly retreating to the far side of the plank made Sarah close her mouth and step away. Racing out the door and along the hallways, she hurried the last of the Woolies into the dyeing room.

"Now it's my turn," said Thomas, pointing Sarah towards the far side of the room. "Get them hidden and help Freck."

With no time for questions, Sarah shooed the children under the maze of drying lines to where Freck and the others crouched behind dozens of huge color vats.

"What's our plan?" asked Sarah.

"We push," said Freck.

"That's not a plan—"

"YOU SLIPPERY LITTLE VIPER!"

As Woolies squashed farther behind the vats, Sarah stepped out for a better view. She spotted Mr. Grim, along with the scar-faced and the earless thugs, chasing Thomas through the drying lines.

Oddly, Thomas didn't look exhausted or alarmed, even when he abruptly turned 180 degrees and whizzed between the two sailors—passing within half an inch of twenty filthy fingernails. Sarah heard the men cursing as Freck pulled her behind a vat.

"Feet on the flat!" shouted Thomas, skidding to a stop beside the next color vat. "FIRST!"

Behind each vat, three Woolies snapped to attention and stood elbow to elbow.

"SECOND!"

Two more Woolies clambered up on the shoulders of the three Woolies to form a higher second row.

"THIRD!"

Again at each vat, a Worm scurried up the backs of the Woolies to stand on the shoulders of the top two Woolies. Sarah couldn't remember seeing squirrels climb as fast as the third row Worms climbed.

"PUSH!"

The human pyramids leaned forward against the vats, and with military precision, every Woolie and Worm grunted and shoved in unison. Sarah grabbed one of the long forks used for twirling the wet yarn from the vats. Holding it like a jousting pole, she pushed it against the smooth vat. But the fork only slipped out of place.

"Sarah, like this!" yelled Thomas, and she turned to see that Thomas also had retrieved a twirling fork. Following Thomas's lead, Sarah jammed the fork under the vat and pushed down with all her weight. The increased leverage worked like magic.

WHOOOOSH!

Perfectly timed with the others, Sarah's vat tipped, and rivers of color blasted the three men. Rabbit-eye pink dripped from Mr. Grim, and eggplant purple so thoroughly soaked the earless sailor that he looked like a six-foot vegetable. The scar-faced sailor kicked and flailed as he swam his way through a torrent of between-your-toes green.

"READY FOR RED!" shouted Thomas, and the sniffling girl and the beet boys stepped forward with their slings. More Woolies marched crisply behind them to form two lines. The second line of Woolies carried armfuls of beets.

The Woolies quickly loaded their slings and swung them over their heads.

Splat! Splat! Splat!

The beets bombarded the raging men, who were sloshing their way to their feet. "Suffering swordfish!" cried the earless sailor as another ripe beet burst apart on his chest.

"Forget the no-leggers," ranted Mr. Grim, turning towards the milkweed girl. "I'll chew your arm off myself." But after his first step, every beet boy pelted the old man until, cringing, he hid behind the two sailors.

"Spiders and spinning wheels!" gasped Sarah as hordes of Woolies swung from the pulleys and lines above. A crew of Tweeners grabbed yarn from the drying lines and swirled about the men like a basket weaver with twenty-eight arms.

The Woolies burst into song as a tangle of string wrapped around ankles and necks and wrists. The men struggled against the tightening noose as Toppers soared overhead and Undies scooted between legs and under armpits. Mr. Grim toppled to his knees, and Tweeners furiously tied knots as they avoided his biting teeth.

The earless sailor flopped on his back, and Sarah heard his moans as Woolies paraded over his belly. She could barely see the scar-faced sailor still standing under a confusion of color. Several Woolies climbed over the man's head and back, but he refused to go down. Sarah swung her giant fork and chopped his knees.

The yelping sailor tumbled into the swamp of yarn, and Woolies swarmed over him with more string. Singing at full volume, Freck somersaulted over the sailor's chest.

"On the quick count!" shouted Thomas, and Woolies scrambled to grab the loose ends of string. "Three—two—ONE!"

The Woolies gave a final yank, and the mesh of colors became a fantastic, if rumpled, rug. Sarah knew that the three grownups must have been somewhere in the woolen garden of happy flowers and dancing insects, but she couldn't piece together whole bodies.

She spotted tiny clues such as fleshy pink skin blended into the blushing rosebushes, or the turquoise-and-silver dragonfly hovering above a wiggling thumb. She wasn't sure whose big toe had transformed into a perfect petunia petal, and she had no idea who owned the bellybutton that replaced the left eye of a ladybug. Someone else's ear quivered like the wing of a sleepy moth. As the men's struggles cascaded like a fresh breeze through the carpet, a cluster of lavender tulips seemed to shake and shimmer with dew.

"He makes a wonderful spindle," whispered Dee Dee, and Sarah laughed as she spotted the earless thug's teary face in the center of a bright yellow daisy.

"He's far more talented than some others," agreed Sarah, pointing to a red-faced Mr. Grim chewing at the snapdragons woven into his beard.

"No time to dawdle," announced Thomas. "We've got to get everyone down the hole."

Sarah grabbed Dee Dee's hand and dashed after the others.

⚓

With the singing Woolies gone from the room, Mr. Grim's head didn't pound quite as much. Only the sobs of two useless sailors echoed off the frosted glass ceiling. Mr. Grim couldn't see his own limbs as they appeared to have melted into the rug, but with each chomp of the wool he felt a little more wiggle room.

"I've had enough," blubbered Huh.

"Quit your boohooing," barked Mr. Grim, spitting a wad of wet yarn into the sailor's daisy face.

"Huh has got it right," sobbed Three O'Clock, also in tears. "Them is yours to deal with."

"I don't need you spineless jellyfish, anyway," muttered Mr. Grim, freeing his shoulders and wriggling the rug down past his waist.

"Jellyfish?" cried Three O'Clock. "If you is smart, you'd get yourself as far as possible from them tiny terrors."

"Them tiny terrors is gonna find out who's boss," hissed Mr. Grim, crawling to his feet.

"Ow!"

Mr. Grim walked over Three O'Clock's arm and stormed out the side exit.

As he stomped through the deserted hallways, Mr. Grim's mind boiled with images of whips and spikes and flames and other glorious means of inflicting pain. "I'll make her suffer," he muttered. "My world was all bliss and buttered biscuits before that wench washed ashore."

Mr. Grim arrived at a fork in the hallway and stopped—

unsure which direction to go. "When I'm done, she'll wish she had drowned. Blimey! I'll grant her that wish myself." Thoughts of Sarah dunked headfirst in the brown barrel, her lungs filling with putrid sheep guts, soothed Mr. Grim long enough to remember that rat of a boy Thomas mentioning a hole.

"The only place for digging holes is in the living string," snarled Mr. Grim, stomping off to the left. He knew that the shortest route to the living string led through the shearing room, and moments later Mr. Grim barged through its doors.

Clap! Clap! Clap!

Baa baa baaaa!

"Outta my way!" fumed Mr. Grim as a rush of four-leggers surrounded him. He spotted Thomas alone at the far doors and shook his fist. "Clap all you want, you little rotter, but I'll be clapping the head off your shoulders."

Clap! Clap! Clap!

Baa baa baaaa!

The giant balls of bleating wool pushed Mr. Grim onto the tile pathway.

Clap! Clap! Clap!

Baa baa baaaa!

Sheep sailed through the air as they bounded over each other's backs and bumped into Mr. Grim. "Stupid four-leggers," he snarled, but his swats were useless against the sheep's thick coats, and the animals continued flying into him and jostling him along the tile pathway. Mr. Grim's hands sank into the warm white fleece as he closed his eyes and scrunched his face against the leapfrogging sheep and the stink of grass.

Baa baa baaaa!

"HOW'D YOU LIKE TO END UP AS MUTTON STEW?" he bellowed.

Baa baa baaaa!

The bleating masked the whir of the cutting blades.

"Ahhhhhhhh!"

Shiny metal flashed by Mr. Grim's beard as he stumbled into the shearing tube.

⚓

In the grass room, Sarah helped the last of the Woolies slide down the hole in the living string.

"Cheeks high," said Sarah, encouraging the final small boy who balked at the sight of the dark shaft. "There's plenty of light in the tunnels."

Thomas tore through the doors, and the Woolie shrank from the hole as the older boy raced through the flock of sheep.

"No dillydallying," Thomas advised, slipping past Sarah and the nervous Woolie. He jumped into the hole, and his next instructions were muffled by several feet of tunnel dirt. "I'll get them organized on the other end."

"See?" Sarah smiled at the boy. "Just follow Thomas, and everything will be wonderful-won—"

WHAM!

The doors swung open, and Mr. Grim plowed into the room. "I swear my next color is gonna be Sarah-black-and-blue," he ranted.

Mr. Grim's half-plucked beard and tattered clothing flapped about him as he shoved sheep aside and stormed towards Sarah. Except for a few clumps of hair, his freshly sheared scalp gleamed in the light. Sarah heard a whimper from the last Woolie, who took one look at Mr. Grim's lunatic eyes—eyes that were minus half their eyebrows—and leapt into the hole.

"I'll kill you twice!" roared Mr. Grim. "I'll rip off your head, sew it back on, and then rip it off again—"

The ram jumping from his pen caught Mr. Grim's attention. "N-nice boy, n-nice boy," Mr. Grim stuttered as the animal snorted and lowered his horns.

Sliding down the hole, Sarah heard pounding hoofs and breathless screams.

"AHHHHHHH! OUMPHF! AHHH! OOWWWW! YIII!"

⚓

On the edge of the shantytown, Woolies spilled from the tunnel like busy ants boiling up from the ground. Everywhere

Sarah looked, Woolies rolled in the grass, or hugged trees, or sang along with the crickets, or licked rocks, or simply laughed as they felt wind on their faces for the first time. The island might have been a bleak landscape of broken-down shacks, but to the Woolies it was a magical new world.

"Why are you doing that?" Sarah asked a tiny Woolie rubbing dirt on her face.

"I want to look like you," answered the girl.

"Oh," said Sarah, remembering how grubby she must be after weeks of crawling through tunnels. "I don't always look so—" She broke off the explanation for a more pressing matter. "No, you shouldn't eat those," Sarah warned a boy munching weeds.

"But when is swallow time?" asked the boy.

"I'm not sure," said Sarah, further distracted by a group of Woolies playing tag on the roof of an old shack. "Please, you must come down from there. Everyone, please, we must go to the shore. We should line up in single file and—" It was no use; the Woolies were too excited for tidy rows. Looking around for help, Sarah spotted Dee Dee. "Where's Thomas?"

"Some Woolies took a wrong turn in the tunnels," said Dee Dee. "Thomas is gathering them up."

"What's that?" asked a Woolie, pointing to the milky disk in the night sky.

"It's the moon," said Sarah.

"The moon," repeated several Woolies in awe, and they reached up on tiptoes trying to touch it.

"It's higher than it looks," said Sarah. "Please, we must get to the shore."

Bong! Bong! Bong!

Woolies drumming on a rum barrel were just a few of the children not interested in Sarah's instructions.

"Shhh, please, we must be quiet."

"It's gone!"

The moon had drifted behind a cloud. The amazed Woolies were full of questions.

"Did it fall?"

"Did it burst?"

"Did it burn out?"

"The moon just went behind a cloud," said Sarah.

"What's a cloud?" asked a Woolie.

"Well, that takes a bit of explaining," said Sarah, and out of the corner of her eye she spotted Freck wandering from the group. "But you'll have to excuse me right now."

After a short dash, Sarah caught up to Freck. "What are you doing?" she asked.

"Look," said Freck, who was weaving about flapping his arms. He pointed to a sea gull swirling overhead. "Isn't it wonderful-wonderful?"

"It's a bird," said Sarah. "Undoubtedly, one of the countless creatures we've woken tonight."

"Can I do the same-same?" asked Freck.

"You mean fly?" said Sarah. "I'm afraid you don't have proper wings."

"Wings?"

"I guess they're like arms with feathers."

"Can I get some feathers?"

"Please, Freck, we should stay close to the others—"

Grrrrrrr.

Sarah spun around and squinted into the night. Low growls rumbled from the murky darkness. As the moon emerged from the clouds, it glinted upon two sets of yellowy fangs. Twenty-five yards away, a pair of shadows took solid shape in the moonlight.

Sarah grabbed Freck's arm and slowly backed away from the mangy beasts, who snarled and bared their teeth. Freck whimpered, and the dogs tore after them.

"Not again," cried Sarah, nearly wrenching Freck off his feet as they scurried across the rutted earth. Their only hope was to climb a tree, but the nearest one stood a hundred yards away. Thick weeds clogged Sarah's strides, and shifting earth absorbed her speed. Behind her, paws pounded the ground at twice the rate of her sluggish feet. Sarah cast a glance over her shoulder and saw the dogs ripping across the grass. A string of spittle flashed silver as it swept back into the night.

"Awwww! Ughf!"

The ground vanished, and Sarah crashed to a halt in collapsed earth. This time she was buried to above her knee. Blinking away tears of pain, Sarah clawed at the cold dirt around her trapped leg. Freck hustled to her side and dropped to his knees. He helped Sarah pull, but her leg remained tightly wedged in the earth.

"Freck, there's no time," cried Sarah as the dogs raced closer. "Save yourself."

Freck stood in front of Sarah, his white Woolie suit glowing in the moonlight. "Four-leggers and two-leggers can be cozy-snug," he cried, raising his thin arms. "Please! We're not jealous of extra legs!"

Ignoring Freck's appeal for harmony, the dogs barreled forward.

A LONG WALK
ON A
SHORT PIER

"RUN, FRECK!" screamed Sarah as the bloodthirsty four-leggers rushed towards them. But Freck only cupped a hand over his eyes and braced for the bone-crushing crash. Sarah couldn't bear to watch, either, and closed her eyes.

"WHSSSSSSSTT!"

A shrill whistle cut the air, and coarse fur brushed against Sarah's cheek. The smell of wet dog lingered and she felt faint, but she also felt alive. She opened her eyes to see Freck taking a brief inventory of body parts—tapping his head, chest, and knees.

Behind her, the dogs rolled at Thomas's feet like a pair of puppies. The Woolies Thomas had collected from the tunnels were happily petting and cuddling the beasts.

"See, Freck," said Sarah with a giddy laugh. "You're very brave."

Freck hadn't located his voice yet, but he smiled with pride. Then he sank to his knees and helped her free her leg. Under the less stressful conditions, Sarah's hands no longer fumbled with the dirt, and she quickly removed the chunks of earth that pinned her knee.

"Let's round up the others," said Thomas, pulling Sarah to her feet.

"Are they afraid of me now?" asked Sarah as the dogs tucked their tails and cowered behind Thomas's knees. Above the dogs' whimpers Sarah heard a squeaking.

"Rodents and rosebushes!" she said.

Nigel was rolling the rusty wheelbarrow across the field.

"Ahoy!" he called, waving. "If you're leaving this wretched island, you'd better bring everyone."

"What's he talking about?" whispered Sarah.

"I haven't a clue," whispered Thomas.

"Can't you set the dogs on him?" wondered Sarah.

"Poor dogs are more frightened than me," whispered Thomas.

Nigel's eyes twinkled in a very unweasel-like way as he approached with his wheelbarrow. "So don't be rushing off," he said. "'Cuz they'd get mighty lonesome without you."

Inside the wheelbarrow, nestled among several blankets, gurgled the three babies from the nursery.

"You freed the puny-news?" gasped Sarah, more astonished than if a sea gull had flown out of Nigel's ear.

"This ain't no place to spend your childhood," Nigel said with a shrug.

"See, Thomas," said Sarah. "What did I tell you about nice grownups?"

"While we're chatting about grownups," said Nigel, scratching his mustache, "would you paint your pa as the forgiving type?"

"I believe my father is in favor of giving a man a second chance," replied Sarah, and Nigel forgot about his mustache and grinned.

Once the other children recovered from their shock of seeing Freck walking hand in hand with a smiling Nigel, it didn't take Sarah and Thomas long to herd the children to the shore.

"Is anyone still on board?" asked Sarah, surveying the cargo ship anchored in the harbor.

"The crew is back inside hiding from you," chuckled Nigel, but he had returned to scratching his mustache and shifting from foot to foot.

"Then why the drooping?" asked Thomas.

"All we got is Pa's old rowboat to ferry the whole lot of you," said Nigel with a wave towards the boat still tied below the pier.

"Maybe we could swim," suggested Thomas.

"Are you crazy?" asked Sarah.

"They swim every day getting bubble scrubbed," said Thomas.

"The ocean is not a bathtub," said Sarah.

"I imagine about eight Woolies can cram in at one time," said Nigel. "And I'd scoot back and forth fast enough."

"Woolies plus Worms plus Sarah plus me . . ." Thomas mumbled as he did the math. "Divided by eight . . . means more than thirty trips!"

"And what happens when we do get on board?" asked Sarah. "I don't see many sea captains among us."

"I told you, Pa taught me to sail," said Nigel. "And you'd better believe you pay attention when Pa is the teacher. Thomas can be my first mate, and the rest of them young'uns will learn quick as a whip, you'll see."

"I knew you was soft," hissed a voice.

"Pit bulls and petticoats!" cried Sarah, whirling around.

Moonlight reflected off Mr. Grim's bald patches as he limped from the shantytown. Where he wasn't tattered and torn, he was bruised and bleeding. He looked as if he had been dug up after three weeks in his own grave.

Woolies and Worms scurried so close together that Sarah felt their quaking fear. Nigel clamped both hands over his forehead as if his brain had exploded. However, Sarah felt Mr. Grim's eyes were more likely to erupt by the way they burned with tiny thunderbolts of blood.

"Get over here, boy," the old man barked at his son. "I'll deal with you later."

"Pa, this ain't right."

"Is your brain turned to glop?" asked Mr. Grim. "Get over here."

Except for his racing Adam's apple, Nigel didn't budge.

"Obey your pa," fumed Mr. Grim. "You hear me, boy?"

Nigel folded his arms across his chest and planted his feet.

"I see you want your thrashing first," growled Mr. Grim, and he started towards Nigel.

"A father is supposed to love and care for his children," said Sarah.

"Missy, you just jumped to the front of the arse-kicking line," said Mr. Grim, veering towards Sarah. "You're a spoilt prissy puss who's gonna get what she deserves." Mr. Grim raised his arm to strike her.

Wham!

Nigel tackled his father, and the children squealed and scrambled away as the men grappled near the water's edge. Mr. Grim squashed his son's face into the muck until Nigel pawed his way free.

Mr. Grim's fist missed Nigel's jaw, and the old man twirled away off balance. Sarah hopped in place, screaming with everyone else as the two men fought like wild animals. Nigel jumped on Mr. Grim's back and wrapped an arm around his neck. The choke hold turned Mr. Grim's face from huff-and-puff pink to stand-on-your-head red. Sarah squeezed her fists tighter—willing her strength to Nigel—but Mr. Grim squirmed enough to bite Nigel's arm, and Nigel's shriek made the children scream even louder. Free, Mr. Grim clawed up a handful of dirt and threw it in Nigel's face.

Nigel staggered about blinking the grit from his eyes.

"Look out!"

Sarah's warning came too late. Mr. Grim's fist smashed into Nigel's jaw, and the children's screams stopped the instant Nigel's limp body hit the ground. Hushed Woolies and Worms trembled while Mr. Grim bent over his unconscious son and caught his breath.

"You're appalling and barbaric and cruel and . . ." Striding towards Mr. Grim, Sarah knew that the entire alphabet would be needed to describe him, "and despicable and evil and fiendish and—"

"What are you doing?" said Thomas, pulling her back.

"I'm about to give him a good poke in the nose," said Sarah, fighting to get loose.

"You'll get yourself killed," said Thomas.

"Oh please, do let her go," said Mr. Grim in a disturbingly calm voice. "I'd enjoy watching the girl pick up her teeth with two broken arms."

Seeing Mr. Grim's thin reptilian smile, Sarah lost her nerve and allowed Thomas to pull her away. She quickly found herself part of a stampede of screaming children bolting down the pier.

"Where you off to?" asked Mr. Grim, leisurely strolling after them. "Can you walk on water?"

The other children had just discovered what Sarah already knew—that a pier doesn't go on forever. Trapped at the end, she found herself beside Thomas and Freck, staring down at the choppy black water.

"Getting back to the tunnels is our only hope," said Thomas.

"How?" asked Sarah.

"Run."

"No."

"Why?"

"He's bound to grab one of us," said Sarah.

"But most of us will get past him," reasoned Thomas.

"No," said Sarah. "We stick together. All of us."

"What's that?" asked Freck, squinting into the harbor.

"The cargo ship?" asked Sarah.

"No, past it," said Freck.

"I don't see anything," said Thomas.

A moonbeam reflected off something white, and Sarah's heart jumped. "It's a sail! Thomas, it's a sail on a ship!"

"Where?"

"Right there," said Sarah, catching another glimpse of the sails.

"I still don't see anything," said Thomas.

"That's 'cuz it's mostly hole-bottom black," said Freck.

"Black?" repeated Sarah.

"Now I see it," said Thomas.

"Oh, it can't be a black ship," moaned Sarah. "Please don't let it be black. Please, please, ple—" Her heart sank as Black Tooth's *London Gorilla* sailed into the harbor.

"What? What's wrong?" asked Freck.

"They're pirates," explained Thomas.

"Will pirates help us?" wondered Freck.

"Pirates don't help anyone," said Sarah.

Standing in the middle of the pier, Mr. Grim taunted the children in his sickly sweet voice. "It's a shame some of you won't be around to meet the next batch of puny-news—"

KABOOM!

Sarah cringed as a cannon blast from the *London Gorilla* lit up the night, and the sea erupted in front of Mr. Grim.

"You fool," raged the old man. "We've no need of pretend fights tonight."

KABOOM!

More flames shot from the ship, and Mr. Grim scarcely had time to curse before the pier exploded under his feet and he flew into the air.

⚓

On the deck of the *London Gorilla,* Lord Tufts adjusted the ropes that bound Black Tooth from his ankles to his chest. Now a prisoner, the pirate could only sulk as Captain Murphy's crew manned his ship. Captain Murphy firing his cannons and looking through his spyglass particularly annoyed Black Tooth. Pirates hate to share.

"Congratulations, Captain," said Lord Tufts. "I've never witnessed such fine shooting."

"Aye, M'Lord," said Captain Murphy modestly. "'Twas nothing."

"If he's such a great shot, how come my pa's not dead?" snarled Black Tooth.

"You've missed the point again, Black Tooth," said Lord Tufts. "Captain Murphy simply intended to stop the threat."

"Doesn't look like a scratch on them youngsters," said Captain Murphy, scanning the children through Black Tooth's spyglass. "But I'm afraid the pier's ripped in two, and they're cut off from—"

Captain Murphy jerked away the spyglass and refocused it. He brought it to his squinting eye again. "Saints preserve us!" he exclaimed, handing the spyglass to Lord Tufts. "My eyes is playing tricks."

⚓

"Calm down," urged Sarah as confusion swept through the trapped Woolies and Worms. "Everyone calm down!" Sarah yelled above the noise, but desperate Woolies, cut off from shore, continued to jostle her. "Please, no shoving." Sarah stepped back and found only air. Teetering with one foot on the edge, she windmilled her arms to struggle for balance. Thomas reached for her, but it was too late.

From the deck of the *London Gorilla*, Lord Tufts saw his daughter plunge into the sea. He flung the spyglass to Captain Murphy, leapt onto the railing, and dove into the harbor.

Left alone on the deck of the *London Gorilla*, Captain Murphy spotted something in the spyglass, and his mouth dropped.

"Well, I'll be an octopus's uncle," he groaned. "He's still kicking." A bald head flashed in the moonlight as the magnified figure of Mr. Grim inched its way up a massive support timber.

"My pa is indestructible," said Black Tooth.

"Not if I put a cannonball in his ear," said Captain Murphy.

"Too bad the rest of my cannonballs is with your stinkin' ship on the bottom of the sea," said Black Tooth.

"He's right, Captain," reported a crewman.

"You can't scrounge up a single cannonball?"

"Sorry, Captain."

"I told ya," Black Tooth gloated. "Pa is indestructible."

⚓

Meanwhile, buried under the ocean's weight, Sarah sank into gurgling blackness as waves heading to shore clashed with waves fighting to rejoin the sea. Strangely, the burning in her lungs began to fade, the cramping in her limbs eased, and her worries floated from her mind. Sarah felt a pillow of sand beneath her cheek, and as her eyelids slipped shut she yearned only for the long blink—a deep cozy-snug forever sleep.

Strong fingers pried Sarah from the ocean floor and flailed her upwards. Surely it was just another undertow of water wrenching at her body. Reluctantly, she opened her eyes. Sarah dismissed her father as one last dream and looked around for Aunt Margaret. Lord Tufts pressed his mouth to hers and filled her lungs. The *whoosh* of oxygen sparked her mind, and she struggled to focus, clinging to her father and clinging to life. Bursting to the surface, Sarah gulped in air between coughs and hugs.

"I knew you'd come back," wheezed Sarah, squeezing her father's neck.

"Shhh," said Lord Tufts. "Save your strength."

"Cockroaches and coffins!" gasped Sarah, pointing to the pier.

⚓

Dee Dee's squeal warned the others, and the children recoiled from the sea monster that leered over the top of a split timber. Mr. Grim gave a grunt and heaved his bloody body up on to the pier. His eyes bulged with fire as he groped his way to his feet and spat out two teeth.

"Shame the brat's father had to ruin a good drowning," seethed Mr. Grim, wiping seaweed from his half beard. "But, luckily, His Lordship can't save all of you." Everyone pressed farther back. "So before they haul me off in chains, I'm gonna toss every one of you sorry beggars into the sea."

KABOOM!

The blast of gunpowder and a sharp howl caught everyone's attention. Mr. Grim looked up and froze as Black Tooth flew through the night sky like a human cannonball.

Thwack!

Sounding like a cat fighting bagpipes, Black Tooth walloped into Mr. Grim, and both men plummeted into the sea.

The harbor exploded in cheers—Woolies and Worms on

the pier, Captain Murphy and his sailors on the *London Gorilla,*
Sarah and her father in the water. Everyone reached for the heavens and hooted and cried. Not sad dreary weeping, but joyous
fountains that made faces glisten in the moonlight. Lord Tufts
wiped his eyes, but more tears came. Captain Murphy's plump
cheeks were soaked. Freck laughed and sobbed at the same time.
It rained such a flood of teardrops that Sarah felt the ocean rise.

THE THIRD PERSON'S
SECOND CHANCE

A FRIENDLY MORNING-PEE yellow sun sparkled on the water, and the gloomy pirate ship was decked out as if for a carnival. Children in fresh white Woolie suits climbed in the rigging, swung on the boom, sang in the crow's-nest, flitted across the deck, and asked a million questions. The crew, delighted by their new passengers, gave as many answers as they could and offered free piggyback rides when they were stumped. Thomas spent his time with Captain Murphy learning about compasses and maps and tides, while Freck discovered that a cannon, if tilted to the proper angle, makes a fabulous slide. Even shy Dee Dee felt cozy-snug enough to ask the cook if he intended to serve turnips during the voyage. Flea had put her up to it.

Sarah and Lord Tufts appeared to be the only somber people on board. It had been a long night; the cargo ship sailors had to be rescued from the shark pit before Lord Tufts sent them on their way with some cold advice about not doing business with unsavory characters. Sarah knew that her father referring to someone as "unsavory" was the same-same as Captain Murphy describing someone as "dirty vermin." Earlier, when the extremely polite mustard-and-cherry-striped giant had been hauled on board in chains, Captain Murphy fumed that he "didn't like sharing a ship with dirty vermin." Captain Murphy then used the phrase "dirty vermin" over eighteen times in one minute. But when Sarah had asked how his own ship had sunk, Captain Murphy grew quiet and his eyes misted over. Sarah only learned that most of the other "dirty vermin" lay on the bottom of the sea with the *Shy Mermaid*.

Huddled near the starboard railing, Sarah and Lord Tufts watched the rowboat that bobbed alongside their ship. A sailor worked the oars to keep the small boat facing into the waves while the last three prisoners were loaded on to the *London Gorilla*. Nigel willingly followed the sailor's instructions, but his father and brother had proven uncooperative. Both Mr. Grim and Black Tooth were gagged and had their wrists bound with rope.

"Father, he's not the same-same," said Sarah. "He's not a frown-maker—honest-honest."

"I beg your pardon?"

"Nigel is not all bad," said Sarah.

"He shall stand trial when we arrive at the new colony," said Lord Tufts. "A trial is more than they all deserve."

"Please, Father, he's sorry for what he's done," said Sarah. "And if it weren't for Nigel's help, I'd hate to think what would have become of us."

Lord Tufts took little time to reflect on the matter. "The man shares responsibility for countless crimes—kidnapping babies being chief among them. He should be locked up."

"The island can be his prison," said Sarah.

Lord Tufts quietly studied the men below.

"Nigel's changed," said Sarah. "And, Father, I've already told him that you are in favor of second chances. What would Aunt Margaret say if you caused a proper young lady to break her word?"

Lord Tufts let out a sigh. "At least he'll have no one left to harm."

"I knew you were an extraordinary man," said Sarah, kissing her father on the cheek.

Lord Tufts raised an eyebrow at the blatant flattery and leaned over the railing to call down to the rowboat. "Release the third man," he ordered.

After a speedy head count, Nigel's face lit up when he realized that Lord Tufts had selected him for freedom. Only Black Tooth's gag held back his curses as he watched his brother returned to the empty rowboat.

"Much obliged, Your Lordship," said Nigel.

"I trust you truly have changed," said Lord Tufts sternly. "And I expect you to rededicate your life to good."

"I certainly will," said Nigel, "I promise. Thank you, Your Lordship—and thank you, Sarah."

"You're very welcome, Nigel," replied Sarah. "And I wish you the best of luck."

"Your Lordship, I too have changed," pleaded Mr. Grim. Having managed to loosen the gag from his mouth, the old man had transformed into a model of innocence. "I've looked into my frail heart, and I swear on my mother's grave—"

"I remember the last time you promised something," said Sarah, and she couldn't resist one final ghost impression. "Wooo wooo, it's scary how fast you can break your word."

"You rotten guttersnipe," muttered Mr. Grim before a crewman crammed his gag back in place. Mr. Grim's tantrum rocked the rowboat, and Sarah guessed that his smothered rant didn't include compliments.

As soon as the prisoners were stowed in the ship's hold, Captain Murphy barked a list of orders, and the crew snapped to their duties. A monstrous chain hoisted the *London Gorilla*'s anchor, and Sarah waved good-bye while Nigel rowed towards what remained of the pier. The other children, oddly sentimental at this parting, gathered at the railing and quietly watched the island grow smaller. Sarah caught Thomas staring at her, and she returned his smile.

"THREE CHEERS FOR SARAH," shouted Thomas.

And the children sang out, "HIP HIP HURRAY! HIP HIP HURRAY! HIP HIP HURRAY!"

"Perhaps I am doing a fair job of raising you," said Lord Tufts, putting an arm around his blushing daughter.

"Oh no, Father," Sarah corrected him. "You're doing a wonderful-wonderful job."

Freck tugged on Sarah's arm and asked in a serious voice, "How many children can share one father?"

"At least this many," answered Sarah, spreading her arms to include the entire group.

Freck's corners rose to his ear tops, but Lord Tufts's eyebrows climbed his forehead as he looked over the throngs of boisterous children.

"Cheeks high," giggled Sarah, and she hugged her father so hard that she squeezed a smile onto his face.

.